Weeping with an Ancient God

Books by Ted Morrissey

Fiction
An Untimely Frost
Men of Winter
Figures in Blue

Nonfiction
The Beowulf *Poet and His Real Monsters*

Weeping with an Ancient God

a novella

Ted Morrissey

✿

illustrations

Adam G. Perschbacher

Includes

A Conversation with the Author, by Beth Gilstrap

Twelve Winters Press

Sherman, Illinois

Published by

Twelve Winters Press, LLC
P. O. Box 414
Sherman, IL 62684-0414

TwelveWinters.com

Weeping with an Ancient God was first published by Twelve Winters Press in 2014.

An abridged version of "A Conversation with the Author" by Beth Gilstrap was published under a different title in *Fourth River* and is used by permission of the author. The same interview appeared in *Men of Winter*, A Revised & Expanded Edition, published by Twelve Winters Press in 2013.

Cover & Interior Page Design: TWP Design
Cover Photo: "Mystic Islands" copyright © Corrie Scott
Author Photo: Melissa Morrissey

ISBN
978-0-9895151-6-0

Printed in the United States of America

For the Author of *Typee*
& for Melissa

contents

acknowledgments

The first chapter of *Weeping with an Ancient God* was published in *The Final Draft* under the title "Melvill in the Marquesas." I would like to thank the following: photographer Corrie Scott for her generosity in allowing me to use her work for the book cover (visit corriescott.net); Fred Lipp for sharing his expertise in antique firearms; John McCarthy for his support of me and Twelve Winters Press; and Pamm Collebrusco for her always reliable editing and proofreading, and also for her support of me and Twelve Winters Press. Furthermore, I thank my sons—Zachary, Ethan and Spenser—for their help, including their help in keeping me humble. Finally, I thank my partner in all things, my wife Melissa, for her unflagging encouragement and optimism.

about the illustrations

Artist Adam Perschbacher mainly had been working on three-dimensional, geometric pieces, but at a couple of his showings he also displayed some drawings. I was immediately attracted to the quality of his eye and the style of his line. Also, I'd had a vague notion of including illustrations with my novella when it would be published a year or more in the future. I approached Adam at a party (at writer Meagan Cass's apartment, I believe) and spoke to him about possibly doing some drawings for my book. He was interested. I shared with him a copy of the manuscript and marked a half dozen or so places that I thought might be fruitful for illustrations. Otherwise, I left him quite on his own (sometimes, I think, to his dismay), trusting that he would come up with something wonderful if left to his own creative instincts. I think it's fair to say that in the beginning I trusted him more than he trusted himself. Here I must gloat that I was right: In the end he did in fact produce something wonderful. His skill, persistence, enthusiasm and professionalism were all brought to bear on this odd project; and I am very much in his debt.

Weeping with an Ancient God

Yet a sailor's life is at best a mixture of a little good with much evil, and a little pleasure with much pain. The beautiful is linked with the revolting, the sublime with the commonplace, and the solemn with the ludicrous.

Richard Henry Dana

Two Years Before the Mast

o n e

~~~~~~

July 13, 1842

Dripping.

It is the dripping and the insensible voices which bring him up from the depths. Darkness and heat. He tries to feel the pitch of the sea, now as familiar as the expansion of his lungs, but there is no movement. Becalmed, he thinks. He cautiously sniffs the air, anticipating the stench of boiling fat. But there is a sweetness instead: thick, oily.

He remembers.

Panic begins to surge in him, like the ocean's surf, like the fever he has had . . . how many days? The number will not come to him. He wants to rise, to step over the darkshape bodies, to run outside, past the dripping cataract to the starlit ocean.

It is all impossible. He heard their cannibal voices; at least two are awake. And Toby? He reaches out and touches the coarse cloth of Toby's shirt and he hears the familiar sleep breathing of his friend. Like so many nights in the belly of the *Acushnet*. The dripping and Toby's breathing take him back for a moment: the roll of the ocean, the stinking blubber, the footfalls above on deck . . . and something else.

Toby moves in his sleep—perhaps he is fitful too—and Toby's hand brushes against his side. He lightly takes hold of Toby's arm, feels the hairs at the wristbone, the slow steady pulse. The rhythm of Toby's blood calms him. He tries to turn toward his friend, to watch his dark outline, but the pain in his leg will not allow it. Shards of agony vibrate through his leg, which has become like wood or stone. He tries to imagine dragging the swollen limb the many miles to the sea. It is impossible.

The cataract and Toby's pulse become synchronous, and Melvill achieves a kind of sleep.

It is daytime when he realizes the old man is talking to him. Melvill is the only one still lying on the floor of the hut, which is rectangular with a bamboo and thatched ceiling about fifteen feet high at its centered apex. Along the walls are baskets, earthen pots, woven mats. Toby is gone. It is unsettling again to see the fading ink on the old man's almost naked body: the bluegreen vines twisting along his still-muscular arms, the disintegrating bluegreen triangle on his forehead, the sinking ovals on his chest that make his nipples dark bull's-eyes. The old man repeats himself for perhaps the fourth time. Melvill understands only two words. "Hermes," the way they have decided to pronounce his name; and "Korykory," the young cannibal who seems to reside in the old man's hut.

Melvill tries to stand but his leg provides him no leverage. He believes he may topple when he feels Korykory lift him to a standing position on his good leg then deftly turn and hoist him onto his back. Melvill is half a head taller and his bare toes nearly drag on the floor. Korykory's wavy brown hair is shaved in arcs over each ear and tapers to a point between his shoulder blades, where the shapes of longwinged birds in flight have been tattooed.

Outside Korykory lifts him higher on his back. Men and women are calmly busy with the demands of the new day. All these many months around the islands of the south Pacific and the stark nakedness of the natives still surprises him. It seems the Typees prefer a short white cloth which hangs from their waist, or even more simply broad waxy leaves. Korykory carries him past the cataract to where the stream is calmer. Melvill is relieved to see Toby floating on his back in the clear water, his bare white chest bobbing like a seaduck among the other dark-skinned bathers. Melvill wants to call out to Toby but he does not want to do anything to provoke the Typees. Half a dozen somber warriors, with long spears and sharktooth necklaces, kneel on either side of the stream.

Korykory takes him beyond the pool of bathers about a hundred yards to a place where the stream begins to pick up speed again. Next to the stream is a patch of high green reeds. Korykory places him at the edge of the reeds and motions for him to proceed in. Melvill is confused. Korykory talks to him with patient meaningless words. Then the native wades into the reeds himself, urging Melvill along. The pliant reeds, which come to Melvill's stomach, snap back after being trod upon. Korykory squats with his back to the swift running water, and Melvill understands. Korykory stands and tries to unbutton Melvill's trousers.

He pushes his hand away, like a bothersome child's. "I'm with you."

Korykory shrugs then moves his tappa cloth aside and urinates a thick stream into the water. The islander waits at the edge of the reeds for Melvill to finish. Korykory points back to the cluster of huts and the bathers. Melvill climbs on and is carried toward the pool. His leg is throbbing from the exertion.

As he is carried along Melvill views the mountains, lavender at their peaks, that Toby and he traversed for three days. This is correct: three days. And the discomfort in his right leg began on the morning of their second day of flight from Nukuheva Bay. By nightfall the discomfort had become the debilitating pain he suffers still. So that is the number that would not come to him: four days of pain. In spite of his bad leg Melvill feels better that his head is clearer now, the fever abated somewhat.

At the bathing pool he sees Toby wrapped in a long swath of the white tappa, like a haphazardly placed toga. The old Typee woman who lives in the hut where they slept is holding the bundle of Toby's clothes and is having an animated dialogue with his friend.

"But, please, I need my clothing, at the very least my trousers." Toby is holding the toga together at the shoulder.

Korykory places Melvill down at the edge of the pool and the old woman gestures at Melvill's checked shirt and duck trousers.

"I believe the witch wants your things too, old fellow," says Toby. "They probably would prefer not to cook us in our breeches—we will be too tough no doubt."

As if she can understand the nature of their conversation, the old woman renews her efforts to explain and screws her face into a foul expression and touches her nose, meanwhile spitting out some Typee expression.

Melvill says, "I believe she is telling us she finds our sailor's smell disagreeable. Perhaps she is offering to launder out the sweat and sea salt."

"Or she intends to burn and bury everything, part and parcel, forthwith. In either case it appears we have no say in the matter."

The stony warriors have formed a loose circle around the four of them, Toby and Melvill, the old woman and Korykory. One of the warriors takes hold of Toby's bare arm and urges him away from the water's edge. Melvill pulls his shirt off over his head then sits on the grassy bank to remove the rest of his clothing. Korykory hands the wad to the old woman and he scoops up Melvill like his new bride and wades into the pool, releasing him when the stream is waist deep.

The water is cool and clean and a great relief to Melvill. The buoyancy relieves much of the pain from his swollen leg. Melvill ducks his head then allows it to bob to the calm surface. The droplets that run from his scalp and ears taste of his own salt. With the temporary relief of his leg Melvill realizes the profundity of his hunger and thirst. For three days Toby and he ate only their ration of a dry mouthful of sea biscuit—"sailor's nuts"—each noon hour. The breadfruits they believed were in abundance beyond Nukuheva Bay were not to be found in the wild mountains. They had agreed to refrain from breaking into ship's stores and risk alerting their mates of their plan to take flight.

Water was also scarce. At the end of their second day in the mountains they discovered a narrow stream. It relieved their thirst, which was terrible and close to undoing them, especially Melvill, who was burdened with fever too. But there was still no food and the biscuit was nearly gone. Also they needed shelter from the sun and periodic rains.

They knew the little stream would lead down the mountain to a settlement—but which natives: the Happars, of whom very little was known; or the Typees, whose cannibalism was infamous throughout the south Pacific? They had no choice but to follow the stream. Turning back was out of the question. The penalty for jumping ship was severe: flogging and treatment befitting a slave for the remainder of the voyage. Their shipmates would not venture into cannibal terrain, no matter what reward was offered by Captain Pease; but a band of Nukuhevas could be easily commissioned for the job. Three or four pounds of Brazilian tobacco and a modest supply of shot and powder would probably turn them out like a pack of red hounds. In the mountains several times Toby and he were startled by a wild boar in the undergrowth which they mistook for a Nukuheva ambush.

Finally, descending from the mountains, they saw a fruitful valley and its huts with steeply pitched thatch roofs. It was midday, the tropical sun high and hard. For a great length of time—Melvill was beyond keeping track of it—they stayed under cover while Toby observed the distant goings on and tried to determine Happar or Typee or some other indigenous tribe. They choked down the last crumbs of biscuit, which seemed to push Toby into a decision. "I must know, old fellow, I must." And he rushed down into the valley. Melvill watched his friend half stagger out of the shadow of the mountain, then he attempted to follow him.

His memory beyond this point is patchy. He recalls falling and struggling up, many times. He is helped—by Toby, he first believes, then realizes it is a girl and boy, dark and naked, on either side of him. Then they are in a hut, the brown faces surrounding them. They are given fresh water (so sweet!) and a kind of citrus mush to eat. "Poeepoee." Toby is attempting to explain who they are and that they have come in peace—which must be obvious from their half-dead, unarmed condition. It is night, the only light from the bluish glow of a taper outside the hut's opening, when Toby and he come to understand that they have arrived in the valley of the Typees. Melvill is too exhausted and feverish to be panicstricken. The knowledge is like a lead weight in his brain, sinking deep as nearly all the natives exit the hut and he and Toby are left to sleep among these cannibals.

After his bath, Melvill, also in white tappa now, is taken to the hut and seated next to Toby at what seems like a place of honor. They sit on woven mats in a corner while a dozen natives eat their breakfast facing them in a semicircle. The hut is spacious, perhaps forty feet by twenty, and the interior walls reveal the simple but sturdy bamboo construction. Here and there pegs protrude from the crisscross of bamboo so that various utensils hang on the walls along with bunches of breadfruits and bananas. Melvill and Toby are each given a bowl of poeepoee plus another of coconut meat and a half coconut shell filled with a citrus juice. Eating with their fingers the tender chunks of coconut are not a problem but the poeepoee is another matter. The day before, starving, they scooped it and poured it like a stringy soup, making a mess of themselves. This morning Marheyo, the old man who is their host, tries to show them the proper technique. Using only one finger he twirls it in the bowl nearly up to the last knuckle until a thick ball of poeepoee is wrapped around; then he sticks the entire finger in his mouth and pulls it out sucked clean. Melvill discovers the technique requires practice.

The natives have begun several conversations and are paying little attention to Toby and Melvill.

Toby swirls his shell of juice before drinking it. "How's the leg holding up?" Toby has raked his reddish blond hair straight back. Like Melvill's, it is long enough to bind in a ponytail. Toby's beard is patchy while Melvill's is dark and thick.

"Not well I'm afraid. Perhaps rest will help." Melvill finishes chewing a chunk of coconut meat. "Why are we receiving service at the captain's table?"

"I can't figure it—unless they are fattening us for the feast."

Melvill had had the same thought. "All this trouble just to murder us."

"The cattleman and the butcher are not a lazy lot."

When breakfast is finished the old woman, Tinor, places all the dishes into a large wickerwork basket and takes them from the hut. Marheyo speaks earnestly to Melvill. The old man repeatedly takes hold of his own right leg, kneading the flesh.

"Yes, my limb is ill," says Melvill, lost.

Marheyo gestures to Toby that it is time to leave the hut with the other guests. The native waves his long brown fingers like he is shooing a cat. When it is just Melvill and the old man together, he speaks emphatically again and points to the mat where Melvill had slept the night before. Melvill understands to move there. Marheyo gently pushes him to a reclining position; and he walks to the hut's opening. Maybe he merely wants me to rest, thinks Melvill, already feeling sleepy. But in a minute or two Marheyo appears to be greeting someone. Melvill watches the old man's back, with its withered fish tattoos, as he speaks to the new arrival about Melvill's leg, all the while massaging his own leg.

A kind of shaman? wonders Melvill.

Marheyo steps aside to let the visitor enter. Melvill is surprised to see a young girl—fourteen or fifteen perhaps—carrying a tortoise-shell bowl. She is the most beautiful island girl Melvill has seen in an ocean filled with vibrant beautiful girls. Marheyo seems to be introducing her. He says her name "Fayaway" several times and each time the old man touches his chest: illustrating her closeness to his heart? Fayaway is thin with long umberblack hair. She appears to be free of tattooing except for two dots at the crests of her upper lip.

Melvill is up on his elbows. Fayaway kneels beside him and puts her hand on his shoulder to urge him to lie flat. There is a bracelet of small blue feathers on her wrist. She moves the tappa away exposing his swollen leg from hip to foot. His skin appears almost phosphorescent in the shaded interior of the hut. The girl gently explores the leg, moving her light fingers over his thigh and knee and shin bone. She and Marheyo speak for a moment. To explain their conversation, Marheyo takes a banana from a bunch hanging on the wall. He uses his bony fingers to show Melvill the yellow skin is smooth and unblemished, then the old man peels the skin and breaks the banana in half, exposing the tiny black seeds inside.

"Yes, there's no outward sign of my distress, no laceration, nor boil, nor prick—so the problem must be inward." He can sense the fever is beginning to overtake his reason again.

Marheyo has a parting word for Fayaway then he leaves his hut eating the banana. It is a bright day and the old man appears to be swallowed by the light.

Fayaway dips her small hands into the bowl and they come out glistening with an oily gelatin. Starting with Melvill's toes she slowly rubs the slick ointment into his skin. Frequently she glances at Melvill's face, perhaps to see if she is hurting him. Melvill is struck by the similarities between her glittering eyes and her half-erect nipples: the same size, the same rich brown. The four perfect circles dance like alien moons in the sky of his feverish mind.

As Fayaway's hands, which are now his entire reality, move past his knee Melvill cannot subdue the sexual arousal he is feeling. He hopes that it is hidden beneath the folds of cloth

but senses it is not. Her hands move over his thigh with the same slow rhythm. At first the ointment was cool but now a penetrating heat has begun at his foot and ankle, and is moving up at the same pace as Fayaway's massaging fingers. When she reaches his hip she gently lifts his leg enough to coat the underside in the gelatin. When she is finished Fayaway instructs him to close his eyes by pointing to them with her slender fingers and closing her own eyes for a moment.

Melvill does as he is instructed. Soon his entire leg is engulfed in the heat. His body is totally relaxed, lifeless, except for his twitching organ, uncomfortable under the folded tappa. He wants to uncover himself to relieve the pressure but senses Fayaway is still at his side. No, not Fayaway . . . Madeline. He believes he can smell the prostitute's pungent city perfume, can feel the irregularities in the feather mattress of her New Bedford boardinghouse room. Then why not pull back the sheet? Propriety is not an issue, only price, and he has what remains of Captain Pease's advance. Eighty-four dollars minus—?

But propriety is an issue for a reason he cannot recall—only its vitalness. And there is the dripping . . . as the icy rain overflows Madeline's clogged gutter. Dripping, yes, but aboard the *Acushnet* now . . . the arousal still pulsating with the heat-rhythm of his leg. The dark figures below deck, the ominous whispering, the ubiquitous stench of the cooking whale sperm. There is the leaden weight of threat on his chest—worse than fear because fear is fleeting. This threat lingers, like a cancer, and there is no escape at sea. . . .

Strong hands are upon him and Melvill strikes out. Once, twice. But his arms are restrained as he is lifted. He wants to shout out but he cannot recall to whom. He finds his captor's face. Korykory. The Typee carries him outside. The sunlight, although partially filtered through the tropical green canopy, is painful to his eyes. Korykory transports him to the bathing pool for the second time that day. He helps Melvill wash the ointment from his leg. In places the gelatin has turned white and cakey. Melvill attempts to hide his buoyant semierect penis.

Still floating, Melvill feels weak but the pain in his leg has subsided. Korykory points to a grove of trees and says something about Toby. Melvill thinks he understands. "Yes, take me to Toby, please." He is helped from the stream, then he covers himself in the white toga and climbs upon Korykory's back. The momentary muscular strain causes the native's tattooed birds to take a single wingstroke. When they are past the boundary of trees Melvill sees a grassy clearing in which there are several huts of varying sizes, including one that is several times larger than the average. Melvill notes that many of these huts are built on a foundation of high stone slabs. Korykory takes him directly to the largest hut, the one that dominates the clearing, and uses footholds that are notched into the stone base to carry Melvill to the entrance. Melvill is amazed at Korykory's vitality. There were strong men on the *Acushnet,* men who could do the heavy work of the sea for hours without tiring; but the strongest among them could not have carried Melvill the distance that Korykory has and then ended the trip with a vertical climb up eight feet of rock.

The front wall of the hut is recessed a few yards so that the stone base forms a portico, which is protected by the extended thatch roof of the hut.

Korykory, only slightly winded, waves his hand before the enormous hut and says, "Ti."

Melvill, balancing on his good leg and Korykory's shoulder, repeats the word and Korykory happily affirms the connection. Korykory suddenly assumes an air of seriousness and seems to resist an impulse to step back. Melvill realizes that a Typee has come from the hut. The man is considerably older than Melvill but is made as muscularly as Korykory or any of the young warriors he has seen. He is richly decorated in tattoos, more so even than the old-man host. He puts his hand on his bare flat stomach and says, "Mehevi." He steps aside and invites Melvill into the Ti. For the short distance Melvill elects to hobble inside with Korykory's support rather than be carried. A tobacco-smoke smell reaches him immediately in the dark hut. The scent is pleasant, although distinct from the cuts of tobacco he is used to. The rich smoke seems to be impeding the adjustment of his eyes. Not quite seeing them, he can sense the dark shapes sitting or reclining on the floor. Melvill has the disconcerting feeling that these shapes are animals peering up at him, wolves and predatory cats. In the entire hut filled with bodies he hears no voices. Perhaps it is his visitation that has caused the Typees' muteness, or it is simply the way of the place.

Korykory is behind guiding him through the clusters of natives.

"Old fellow, there you are!"

Melvill, relieved, can hear the relief in Toby's voice too. Korykory helps him to a mat by his friend.

"I was afraid they'd decided you would be the appetizer and I the main course." Toby is holding a short wooden pipe.

Mehevi has sat facing them. From a basket he produces a pipe similar to Toby's. It is already stuffed with tobacco. Toby takes a small stick and puts one end into the bowl of his own pipe until the tip is glowing orange; then he uses it to set off Melvill's pipe.

Melvill inhales deeply and lets the warm smoke out of his mouth and nose. "A tad rough but a godsend nonetheless."

Toby nods. "Must be a local leaf."

Melvill notices the murmur of conversation throughout the hut. Apparently the silence was a reaction to his arrival.

"How's the leg now, old fellow?"

"Perhaps a bit more limber but still a fount of pain. My physician is lovely, but I'm afraid I may need less primitive doctoring."

"I'm afraid we may yet become the guests of honor at a Typee feast."

Mehevi, who has been smoking silently, smiles and says, "Typee," his white teeth aglow in the shadowy Ti.

Melvill's eyes have adjusted finally so he scans the interior. There are dozens and dozens of Typees, young men and old, all sitting or reclining with their pipe; on woven mats that are either rolled into cushions or flat on the cool stone floor. They are in groups of four to six or seven, carelessly arranged. Ever since entering the Ti Melvill has been sensing dark circular objects hanging at regular intervals on the walls. With his improved vision he looks up to discover the dark shapes are human heads. The pipe nearly falls from his lips. "Toby . . . on the walls."

Toby glances up for an instant. "Yes, quite a pleasant decorating touch isn't it?"

The faces look to have the texture of smoked meat, desiccated and shrunk close to the bone. The eyes have been replaced with something white and iridescent, chipped stone or seashell. The heads glare wildly from their mounted positions. Melvill thinks perhaps they retain the shadow of their horrorstruck expression at the instant of death.

Mehevi must notice Melvill staring and he gestures toward the heads and offers an explanation. The only word that Melvill understands is "Happar," the Typees' neighboring enemies.

Melvill says to Toby, "Perhaps this Ti is one large hunting lodge and these heads the cherished trophies."

"Yes, and a men's club as well."

They spend a peaceful hour in the Ti with their pipes and the indistinct native voices. From time to time Melvill can imagine that the voices are mumbling English, the meanings just beyond his comprehension. Also, the displayed heads start to become as familiar as sconces. Even though there is no signal that Melvill can detect, all at once the Typees extinguish their pipes and begin to herd outdoors. Melvill and Toby follow suit, Melvill with Korykory's quick assistance.

The women and children have come to the grove and set up a midday meal. Korykory takes Melvill and Toby to a spot where the old couple, Marheyo and Tinor, are waiting with the meal.

They sit on sheets of white tappa in the grass in the narrow shadow of the Ti. The meal is the same as breakfast except for the substitution of coconut milk for the citrus juice. Melvill is surprised at the number of Typees who are having their meal in the grove. It is an aboriginal scene, unchanged in hundreds of years, perhaps thousands. But their time is limited, speculates Melvill. He thinks of the three French men-of-war anchored in Nukuheva Bay, and of how the occupation has already changed the coastal region of the island, and of how the French will not be satisfied with only the coast and will systematically work their way inland. He thinks of how the Christian missionaries will follow the French like the scavenger sharks in the wake of the *Acushnet*.

"This certainly is superior to starvation," says Toby after sucking poeepoee from his finger, "but I keep thinking about sinking my teeth into a thick beefsteak."

"One day soon I'm certain—when we reach the Hawaiian Islands." Melvill hears the skepticism in his voice.

Melvill wants to stand when Fayaway approaches but his leg will not allow any sudden movement. The beautiful girl speaks to Marheyo and Tinor then she says something to Melvill—he guesses about his leg. Before he can find a way to respond she picks up a large bowl of boacho and offers it to him. Melvill points to his smaller bowl which contains the fruity mush. Fayaway insists that he take more.

Toby says, "I believe the doctor is prescribing a remedy, old fellow."

Melvill pours the yellowish boacho into his bowl. "Thank you."

Fayaway continues kneeling at Marheyo's side talking to the old man. In profile, with her dark hair spilling over her shoulders, she appears totally nude.

Toby runs his finger along the rim of his bowl. "Aside from the distinct possibility of ending up as sustenance, the Marquesas have their redeeming qualities."

Melvill does not comment.

When the meal is finished Tinor and Fayaway load the empty bowls into the large basket, placing the folded tappa on top. A majority of the men, including the decorated Mehevi, saunter toward the Ti. Melvill, weary, mounts Korykory's back thinking the Ti is their destination too; however Korykory begins following Marheyo, who is walking directly away from the massive hut.

"Where are we going?" Melvill watches over his shoulder as Toby stands hesitant for a moment then shrugging turns toward the Ti.

Korykory must sense the meaning of Melvill's question and offers a lengthy but fruitless Typee reply. Not bridging the gap with the old man they follow, Korykory takes a path out of the ring of huts; and Melvill discovers that beyond the grove about a third of a mile are dozens of small flat-roofed structures. Each one they pass has a totem of carved stone blocking its black opening. Many of these small huts are in disrepair and collapsing in on themselves. Several of the totems have fallen over. Another footpath to the left and they come to a hut which is under construction. Korykory unloads Melvill near a log on which he can rest then Korykory and Marheyo begin working on the bamboo-reed hut. They work without speaking, each knowing his part in the process. Korykory uses a sharp-edged stone to snap the bamboo at the proper length. The reeds are slightly larger around than a man's thumb. Marheyo skillfully lashes the bamboo together with vines to extend the second wall. The first wall stands erect supported by thick tree limbs; the wall being built is approximately a third of the first wall. Each is about six feet high, estimates Melvill. He is surprised that Korykory uses such a primitive method to size the bamboo because Melvill has noticed metal blades and tools among the Typees—evidence of some contact, if only indirectly, with sailors.

The spot where Melvill has been placed is shady and

drowsiness soon begins to overtake him with the rise in his fever again. He waits quietly hoping that Korykory will finish his part and return him to Marheyo's hut, or at least the Ti. But Marheyo and Korykory work without pause and there are so many dozen bamboo reeds to be sized.

Melvill hobbles a short distance to a grassy place near the log and lies down. The grass feels cool and soft, and soon Melvill is asleep. The snapping and lashing of the bamboo enters his sleepworld to become the sounds aboard the *Acushnet*: the reeving of the sails, the banging of the tackles against the masts, the securing of supplies below deck. And there is something missing . . . some*one* missing. Melvill watches the search boats circling astern, gray boats on a gray sea, and Melvill knows the truth. He believes he knows.

When Melvill awakens Fayaway is sitting on the log watching Marheyo and Korykory work. The change in light filtered through the leafy canopy—now more yellow than white—tells Melvill it is late afternoon. Fayaway smiles down at Melvill then speaks to the silent workers. She says the name "Hermes" and she uses the word "kiki," which relates to food or eating, Melvill has learned.

Melvill tries to raise himself and finds that the pain in his leg is less acute but the stiffness is profound—truly like a piece of driftwood. He cannot bend his knee at all, barely his ankle. Fayaway, seeing his difficulty, calls to Korykory and the two of them help Melvill to the log. Melvill notices the differences in their grip on each bare arm: Korykory's hands are callused and powerful; Fayaway's small and light, like a bird's wings.

While Melvill and Fayaway sit she is explaining something about the structure being built. Marheyo *this*, she says, and Marheyo *that*. The second, or back, wall is erect and the third wall is a quarter finished. Marheyo and Korykory are tidying up their materials, wrapping the bamboo into long palmetto leaves, balling the vines. When they are finished, Korykory readies himself to carry Melvill, who feels a pang of guilt at not being able to walk. After all, Korykory has been laboring all afternoon and now he must carry Melvill the great distance from the secluded flat-roofed huts, past the grove with the Ti, and back to the cluster of huts where Marheyo and Tinor live near the waterfall. There is nothing to do about his guilt. Marheyo and Fayaway walk in front, Korykory with Melvill behind. Fayaway, though tall for a Typee female, comes only to Marheyo's shoulder, and the old man is somewhat stooped. Their bare feet leave no trace on the hard earth.

The grove where they lunched is quiet. Melvill believes there must be dozens of men in the Ti smoking and socializing but he sees no one near its black entrance. It is as if the entire grove is sleeping—even the huts and the wildlife—or holding its breath, suspending living for a time. The quiet makes Melvill uneasy. He wants to ask, "Where is everyone?" but anticipates no response. Half dozing on Korykory's back, Melvill recalls legends of magic spells putting entire villages to sleep, of evil palls cast upon castles. Always it is an heroic act which lifts the spell. He senses no heroism in himself nor in Toby. Desperation, trepidation, primal fear—just beneath the surface.

As they approach Marheyo's hut Melvill sees Tinor and other old women bent over a large piece of white cloth working it with some sort of hand tool, like a small rolling pin. They are chattering but stop as soon as Marheyo's group draws near. Marheyo speaks briefly to his wife, or so their relationship seems to Melvill, before Korykory takes Melvill inside. Fayaway continues past Marheyo's, presumably to her family's hut.

Korykory eases Melvill down then immediately goes to a corner of the hut and lies in a fetal position. In seconds, while Melvill is still watching, Korykory is asleep. At first, in the dim light, Melvill does not recognize the things stacked on his sleeping mat but touches them and realizes they are his clothes. He is happy to get out of the makeshift toga and put on his familiar shirt and underbreeches and trousers. They are freshly laundered and have a pleasant floral scent. He leaves his shoes and stockings on the mat.

Melvill sits, thinking that is all he will do, but the drowsiness of fever quickly overcomes him and he lies down. He recalls sleeping in a strange room with his older brother. It is Christmastime and outdoors a thick blanket of snow covers the ground. Melvill hears his father's voice . . . downstairs, talking and laughing—storytelling. Melvill reaches for his old patchwork quilt but it is not cold really. His groping hand finds the white tappa and he covers himself. His father's story is a dissipating echo, like invisible dripping in a cave. He tries in vain to revive the dream of New England, to resurrect the ghost of his father. The darkness of the cave becomes real when Melvill awakens. The hut is black. He sits upright and looks at the opening. It is a rectangle of lavender twilight. Korykory is gone. Melvill struggles up and goes to the opening. No one is outside. From Marheyo's hut Melvill can see the grove with the Ti and between the blacktrunk trees is the orange glow of fire. Supper time? he wonders. Then why was I not called? And where is Toby?

Because of his leg, the Ti seems a great distance but Melvill begins to make his way. He is surprised that the ground is cool under his bare feet. He expects it to feel like baked terracotta, only minutes from the kiln. Walking is painful and he wishes he had a sturdy stick. He can detect the smell of woodsmoke now and of roasting meat. He thinks of Toby, whom he has not seen for hours. Queasiness slows his already slow pace. The light from the fire in the grove reminds him of the bellies of the cookstoves on the *Acushnet*, day and night boiling down the blubber when a kill has been made. The sickening smell of the melting fat, which permeated every space on the ship, comes to him again, adding to his nausea.

The light of the fires—the one in the grove and the recollected fire from the ship—nearly blinds him. Melvill stops, as if the twin fires have consumed his energy, his will. It is all he can do to keep from falling to the ground.

The Typees who emerge from the grove are like two shadow-warriors: black shapes against the fireglow. Melvill wants to run but cannot. He collapses when the dark figures reach him. Each taking an arm and a leg they carry him to the grove. Melvill, sick with fear, tries to shout out—for Toby, Korykory, Fayaway—but he has no voice. In the grove he sees that it is not one great fire but many fires. Their heat, combined with the sultry tropical heat, is intense. The warriors, who at least have distinct features in the firelight, carry him to one of the smaller ground-level huts adjacent to the Ti.

"Old fellow!" Toby rushes over. "I had really given you up." He helps Melvill to sit upright. They are alone in the small dark hut.

"What's happening?" Melvill's voice is a hoarse whisper.

"I can't say for certain. They've been dancing about these fires for some time—rather ceremoniously."

Melvill leans over to see out. "Is the ceremony for us, do you think?"

Toby rearranges himself so they are on either side of the hut's opening. "I can't say; but it seems likely."

"Why not get on with it then?"

"It is their religion, I suppose. You know that religious rites are not known for their swiftness."

"Toby, you must escape. I'm in no condition to flee, but you …"

"My chances out there are no better, especially in the dark. There are hundreds of them. Thousands maybe. The whole damned cannibal nation has turned out for the event."

They sit in silence for a time. Outside the fires crackle and the Typees dance and chant. Melvill wonders about the decisions they have made, jumping ship and setting out for the wild country with no provisions and no weapons—totally at the mercy of who or what would find them. The whole episode makes no sense. There is no logic to any of their moves. Melvill, the gifted student, the debate society president, is awed by the rashness of his actions. He and Toby were doomed the instant they left Nukuheva Bay—running in that torrential downpour like freed schoolboys.

"I'm sorry it has come to this," says Melvill.

"It's not your fault, old fellow. We made the plans together. I knew what the possibilities were." Toby glances outside. "They're coming."

Their hands clasp on the sandy floor of the hut.

Melvill recognizes one of the trio approaching as Korykory. Another is Mehevi, the richly tattooed chieftain. The third Typee, who stays close to Mehevi's side, Melvill does not know. All three, backlit, appear to wear plumes of fire for headdress.

Korykory kneels at the hut's opening. He holds a flat piece of wood. He says something "kiki."

"They bring food," repeats Melvill.

On the wood are several strips of smoking meat.

"Yes," says Toby, releasing Melvill's hand, "but my god, what kind of meat?"

"Kiki," insists Korykory thrusting the strips toward Melvill.

Melvill's stomach is turning, partly from the fear that has been consuming him and partly from the idea of this cannibal offering. He recalls the severed heads in the Ti. "No kiki," he says weakly, shaking his head.

Korykory seems confused, almost embarrassed. He takes a piece of the meat and bites it himself. "Puarkee." He grins and chews the meat; juice trickles down his chin. "Puarkee." He holds the remainder of the meat to Melvill's lips.

Melvill, his head pounding from the tension and the fever, hesitates then opens his mouth slightly. Korykory pushes the meat past Melvill's parted lips. He fights the urge to gag as he begins to chew. The rich flavor floods his tongue and it is familiar. He swallows some of the meat. "Pork. The natives are roasting some of those wild boars. It's delicious."

Korykory, visibly happy, turns to Toby, who takes a strip of meat. He cautiously puts it in his mouth. "You're right—

damned succulent too."

They come from the hut and sit near one of the fires. The Typees dance and chant and tell their incomprehensible warrior stories. The halfmoon is high when the feast finally ends.

t w o

~~~~~~

The next day begins in the same manner: toilet and bathing at the stream then breakfast. Melvill is more at ease, more confident the Typees do not intend to murder them. Toby must feel better too. He is ravenous at breakfast, which includes a type of dried nut in addition to the poeepoee and juice. After, Marheyo ushers everyone from the hut except Melvill, who knows to go to his mat. In a few minutes Fayaway is there with the tortoise bowl and ointment. She smiles when she greets Melvill and says the word "leg."

"Yes leg. My leg seems a bit improved today." Melvill is delighted at Fayaway's use of the English word, though she pronounced it nearly like *league*.

Fayaway attempts to unbutton Melvill's trousers but her fingers are not used to buttons. Melvill assists her and exposes his leg, pulling down the pant leg and raising up the baggy right leg of his knee-length breeches. Fayaway begins her inspection then the application of the ointment, first to his toes and foot. She seems to linger there. Melvill thinks about the extreme arousal he experienced before and wonders if Fayaway's hesitation is due to that. Or perhaps he is only imagining her reluctance. His speculation ends momentarily when Fayaway moves on to the ankle bone and calf. Melvill tries to distract himself from the sensations, to avoid the embarrassing and uncomfortable arousal. First he thinks of what his family must be doing now—his brother at work in the shop, his mother sewing or cooking—but these images depress him. The homesickness is heavy on him until his mind switches to the whaler, particularly the hunt, which was exhilarating. It was the killing he despised because it was such a waste, and the horrific carving up of the massive carcass afterward, knowing that the ship would be rife with the noxious odor of boiling fat. Melvill sees the blood flowing on the *Acushnet*'s deck: a scarlet river to and fro with the pitching of the waves. Then he sees young Jones, younger even than Melvill and come from New York City too, at first smiling, working on deck, singing out a sailor's work song, then how he must have been at the last, struggling in the icy grip of the ocean, sucking down the brine, eternally sinking sinking . . .

Fayaway's hands move to his thigh, each finger in its own synchronous elliptical motion, its own small penetrating orbit. Melvill's erection pulsates within his thin breeches. He looks at Fayaway to see if she notices but she appears absorbed in the massage. The muscles in her shoulders twitch with exertion. She stops with one hand for a moment to sweep a strand of hair behind her ear and accidentally highlights her cheekbone with the glistening ointment. Melvill reaches up and wipes it away with his thumb. He allows his fingertips to hesitate for a moment at her ear.

Fayaway, at first startled by his action, seems now self-conscious. She hurries in her way to finish anointing his leg. She casts her beautiful eyes down, to her hands. The moment she finishes she is gone. Melvill stares at the thatched ceiling as the ointment's heat overtakes his leg. Today its radiance seems to go beyond the skin that Fayaway touched—to his stomach and his other limbs, and to his chest where his heart beats against the hard-earth floor.

It takes Korykory a long time to retrieve him for his second bath. Even the stream's bracing water does not cool the burning in his soul. It is all too much: their escape from the whaler, the trek through the mountains, their encounter with the cannibals, the lovely Fayaway. Floating in the bathing pool Melvill cannot concentrate; his mind is all skittering emotion.

He is startled to hear his name, his real name. Toby is standing on the bank of the stream holding two pieces of wood, one long, one cut short.

"The life of luxury must be enthralling. I thought for an instant you were drowned there in the water." Toby makes a T shape with the wood. "Look here, old fellow, at what your footman and I have been about this morning. I have been lent some tools—for lack of a more apt description—and we are fashioning you a crutch." Toby places the disassembled wood under his arm to show that it is the proper height. "By noon you should have it—and some measure of independence as well. I'd be finished in a quarter hour if I could get at the carpenter's cabinet on board."

"I appreciate your efforts," says Melvill from the pool, "but what I truly need is to be free of this affliction."

"Yes I know. I've been thinking about that." Toby pokes the crutch stick into the ground. "Surely there is a physician among the French. With three men-of-war they would've packed one of those, would they've not? They brought the admiral's damned horse—why not his damned doctor too?"

Melvill recalls the brightly uniformed Frenchman riding his white horse on the beach, to the amazement of the Nukuhevas, who seemed to think it was some sort of overgrown pig. "It seems likely. But would the *Acushnet* have set out yet?"

"Pease intended to by now. I can't imagine he would hold his departure on our accounts."

"No." Melvill is feeling lightheaded again.

"I must learn what the best route to Nukuheva is. Certainly not by way of the mountains as we came."

Korykory, sitting on his haunches at the edge of the bank, becomes more alert at the word he understands, Nukuheva.

"I'm afraid it doesn't matter. Even with the crutch I would be hard pressed to go only a few miles, and it must be eighteen or more to Nukuheva Bay by coast, and heaven only knows what sort of terrain lies between here and there."

"I wasn't suggesting, old fellow, that you would go. That is clearly out of the question. I would go then come round for you by boat—surely I could secure one for the purpose at Nukuheva."

Melvill tries to consider the proposal but has difficulty focusing. "Would the Typees even let you leave?" The stonefaced warriors are still dogging Toby, ominous in their silence.

"I don't know. Well, first things first." Toby turns away with the crutch pieces.

After his bath, Korykory takes Melvill to the place where Marheyo is building his small hut. It is mid morning but the forest gives the sunlight a duskiness. Melvill sits on the log hoping Fayaway will come to him. He wishes he already had Toby's crutch. He could at least explore along the path of small huts, which winds like a serpent through the tropical forest. He senses there is a holiness about the huts, like broken and abandoned shrines or temples.

Yesterday the snapping and lashing of bamboo was hypnotic; today it is merely annoying. Melvill feels restless and irritable. He tries to concentrate on the natural sounds: on the wind high above in the forest canopy, on the squawking of the painted birds, on the clatter of the invisible insects. He conjures the erotic image of Fayaway, then of other maidens he has known. He envisions the congested seaport at New Bedford, the clippers and whalers and other tall ships. Nothing eases his restlessness.

Marheyo's and Korykory's work-trances are finally broken when another Typee arrives along the path. They greet him warmly with smiles and pats on his muscular arms. He is between Marheyo and Korykory in age. His head is completely shaved and around its crown is a tattooed garland. He is holding an object wrapped in white cloth which Melvill at first mistakes for a baby because he is cradling it as gently and as lovingly as a father would his infant. After a brief exchange between the three, the Typee unwraps the cloth to reveal a stone statue—

similar to the ones at the entrances to each of the small huts. It reminds Melvill of a skrimshander, a figure that some whalemen carve from whalebone. Marheyo takes the primitively carved statue as if it is his child. Melvill notices that the statue's arms have thin lines etched into them, like Marheyo's vine tattoos. And the stone idol has the twin bull's-eyes on its chest; and an exaggerated version of Marheyo's wide flat nose. Clearly the statue is of Marheyo and the old man seems quite pleased with it. Melvill is surprised to see both Marheyo and Korykory brush aside tears.

When Marheyo is finished examining the statue, he hands it back to the Typee artisan—a father returning his child to the midwife—who then wraps it in the cloth again and takes it away.

"So that's what you're building here," says Melvill, "a sort of tomb for Marheyo."

The old man turns to Melvill and nods deeply, almost a bow, but no doubt only at the utterance of his name.

"And the rest of these huts are for departed warriors."

Marheyo and Korykory are returning to their work.

Melvill wonders at the dilapidated condition of most of the bamboo tombs and at the stone idols that have fallen. Perhaps it is "taboo"—a word used by the various bands of natives throughout the islands, relic of some common ancestral language, long forgotten—for the living to do anything with the tombs other than construct them. To Melvill it seems reasonable to allow the natural world to take its course with the tombs without human interference. Yet these huts are well protected from the rains and the ocean winds. The tropical forest even filters the corrosive salt from the air. Some of these shrines are probably centuries old, he thinks.

Marheyo and Korykory—father and son, Melvill is certain now—have returned to building the hut in earnest silence. One bamboo reed at a time. Lashed together one upon the next like the days of our lives, thinks Melvill, constructing an edifice of testimony. He wishes he had pencil and paper.

The discomfort in his leg, exacerbated by the treatment, is becoming acute. He waits, only half alert, for Marheyo and Korykory to finish their morning work and return him to the grove for the noon meal. By the time they do start back Melvill feels sick and weak. Korykory seems to infer his condition and carries him with extra care. A gentle rain trickles through the forest ceiling. There is no one lunching in the grove so Korykory carries him on toward Marheyo's hut. Looking over Korykory's shoulder Melvill sees Toby and Fayaway near the hut's entrance under the narrow cover of the protruding roof. A sound reaches Melvill that he has not heard before: it is Fayaway's laughter. Toby is entertaining her by making odd faces and clowning with the crutch he has fashioned. Melvill's overall pain is replaced by a wave of jealousy.

Toby calls out when he notices them. "Old fellow, look here." Toby places the crutch under his right arm; it is a bit too tall for him and his shoulder is hunched, which further amuses Fayaway.

Korykory sets Melvill by his friend. Melvill almost feels too weak to balance on his good leg.

"You look terrible. Here." Toby offers him the rough-hewn crutch.

It does help Melvill stay upright. "Thank you. This seems very sound indeed." Melvill makes his way inside. He does not look at Fayaway. He does not want to see the shadow of a smile still lingering on her lips.

Melvill is too ill to eat so he sleeps in a corner while Marheyo's family and Toby have their lunch. When Melvill awakens his hunger is severe. He devours three bananas and a tangerine while Tinor prepares a bowl of boacho. They are alone in the hut. Bands of sunlight slip through the few separations between bamboo reeds. While she prepares the food, Tinor speaks to him in maternal tones. Occasionally she smiles and touches the flesh on her face.

"Is my color improved?" guesses Melvill. He feels healthier, more energetic, and the throbbing in his leg has ceased.

After his second bowl of boacho Melvill is revitalized. Using the crutch he goes outside. There is a group of women polishing the insides of coconut shells. Melvill cannot help noticing the rhythmic swaying of their breasts. Nearby children are playing a game with seashells and small stones. No one takes notice of Melvill. He is not practiced with the crutch but the feelings of independence and mobility are uplifting. He makes his way to the cataract and stands so close that invisible drops of cold water peck at his face and neck. It is glorious. Leaning against a boulder he removes his shoes and shirt and trousers, leaving only his breeches. He carefully crawls over the boulder and the wet rocks, then he reclines in the swift running water and lets it bubble over his head and shoulders. It leaps at his ears and between his callused fingers.

Out of habit he sniffs for the scent of salt but there is only verdant freshness. Melvill is fading into a dreamy state . . . when Tinor's screeching startles him to full alertness. The old woman is pointing her skeletal finger at him and spitting out a cascade of Typee words. The only one Melvill catches is "taboo . . . taboo!" Melvill scrambles back to the bank and begins pulling on his clothes. More patiently Tinor tries to explain what is wrong. She gestures downstream to the bathing pool and farther to the toilet area. Tinor points to the cataract and pantomimes drinking.

"I'm sorry. I didn't realize one couldn't enter the stream here. I'm sorry." Melvill bows to communicate his apology.

Tinor slaps him on the shoulder and turns shaking her head, seeming amazed at his ignorance.

Melvill returns to the cluster of huts. Tinor is disappeared. He assumes she is inside again. Balancing on his crutch, he calls to the women working the coconut shells: "Do you know where my friend is? Do you know where Toby is? Toby?"

The women stop for a moment, stare at Melvill and giggle;

then return to their work.

"Thank you for your help."

One of the children looks up from her game and motions toward the grove. The naked little girl smiles shyly at Melvill, motions again, and concentrates again on the game.

The grove seems too far, especially with the throbbing ache beginning to return to his leg. But the idea of Toby's company and perhaps smoking a bowl of tobacco in the Ti is very appealing. Slowly he starts to make his way. The crutch digs into the sandy ground.

When Melvill reaches the edge of the grove he sits under a palm tree to rest. The shade is cool and moist. From his position he can see the side and the rear of the Ti, and the smaller huts beyond, and two of the paths that lead out of the grove—one curls into the forest toward the warriors' tombs, the other he does not know, maybe to the sea, which is several miles. The sea. The great conundrum. The freer of minds and souls and the enslaver too. The great greenblue giver of life and dealer of death. Mystery and faith and fear. And all the seamen are either friend or enemy. There is no indifference. Even the sea's animals choose sides—giving themselves up freely to sustain you or fighting you to the death. Melvill recalls the story of the gray whale with the white patch—"Mocha Dick" the sailors of the southern seas called him—who had destroyed thirteen boats and took the lives of more than thirty men.

"Old fellow . . . I nearly tripped over you." Toby helps him to stand. "Look what our little brown flower has given me: a map of the whole damned island."

Melvill touches the old faded parchment which is crumbling at the edges. It smells of the sea, and of decay. Nukuheva is clearly rendered with its volcanic peaks, streams and coves. The valley of the Typees is recognizable. But there are great patches of emptiness where the anonymous cartographer had no knowledge of the island.

"Cook himself may have drawn the map," says Toby.

Nukuheva

8°52'S 140°08'W

"Judging by its age it was more likely a Peruvian hand which sketched it. And its lack of scale suggests that much is based on hearsay and not firsthand knowledge." Melvill runs his finger along the island's coastline. "Here must be Nukuheva Bay."

"Right, and these the mountains we traversed, and this the stream we followed down." Toby points toward the stream itself, just out of view from the trees. "And look here, this appears to be a path, due east out of the valley then south—probably along the base of that mountain." He points to the farthest peak.

"A path, or a national border. And how far—and how treacherous? You're not risking your neck on my behalf."

"It's not solely on your behalf, old fellow. I have no intention of living out my days among these cannibals." Toby studies the crude map for a moment. "I would think I could complete the journey in three days or perhaps fewer. If luck is with us, we'll be sailing for the Hawaiian Islands in a week's time."

"I shall try to adopt some of your optimism." Melvill studies the half dozen warriors who have been twenty yards from them. Their silence and their omnipresence, like creeping jungle vines, must make it possible for Toby to disregard them.

"Where were you headed, old fellow, before I came upon you here?"

"To the Ti, to find you and perhaps have a pipe."

"A splendid idea. There's not much I can do in preparation. In the morning I shall avail myself of some fruits and fresh water and set off. If those dressmaker's dummies intend to keep me here, I suppose this will be the perfect test to see."

Melvill is anxious about Toby's planned departure. Throughout the remainder of the day the same thoughts eat away at him like an abscess: What if Toby is not allowed to leave and they are in fact prisoners here? What if Toby leaves and is never heard from again? Perhaps the Happars will kill him, or the Typees in secret. What then? Melvill will be left totally alone among these cannibals. What if Toby reaches Nukuheva Bay and Captain Pease is not departed and Toby is placed under maritime arrest? Or what if Toby has the opportunity to sign on with a crew bound for Hawaii? After all, how well does he know Tobias Greene? Is eighteen months enough time, no matter what the circumstances, to form these kinds of bonds? Toby is offering to risk his life twice for Melvill—first by traveling out of the Typee Valley, then by venturing back into it.

That night Melvill is again fitful in his sleep, in an ague of worry, his leg ailing. He reaches out, as on the first night with the Typees, to feel Toby next to him. Toby is turned on his side, his back to Melvill. Toby has gone to bed shirtless and his bare white skin is like a spirit in the dark hut: the ghost of some fallen warrior, whose head hangs on display in the Ti. His feverish mind imagines the heads having an animated discussion in the abandoned Ti, telling the tales of their deaths, blinking furiously over their iridescent mother-of-pearl eyes. Melvill thinks he can hear the murmur of their voices on the wind. The murmur becomes the beating of waves on rocks. Sea spray explosions. Again and again. Bursting. The memory of the *Acushnet* coming into Nukuheva Bay and the natives racing to greet them in their long canoes. The beautiful young girls leaving a trail of flower petals in their wake: floating paths of yellow, lavender and pink. And all the young girls are Fayaway, their molten eyes beckoning like the Sirens'. The horny sailors twitching at their posts.

The whole wild show threading its way between the French men-of-war anchored offshore. Dark sentinels in the bright bright day.

Toby is gone. Melvill searches the hut in the blue predawn light. Awkwardly he gets up with the crutch and avoids falling over the sleeping bodies. Outside he nervously looks for his friend and finds him sitting on a rock gazing at the cataract and stream. Toby is still only half dressed. Melvill comes up from behind and breaks his reverie.

"Thought perhaps you had already stolen away."

"Oh no. It was the strangest thing—I thought I heard

something out here . . . well it sounded like a cat's meowing."

"A cat? All this way inland?"

"Yes, odd, isn't it?" Toby stands and stretches, making his ribs even more pronounced in the shadowy blue light. "No, I'm not leaving until after breakfast. I'd like to get an earlier start but it may be the last meal I'll have for some time."

The tips of the mountains to the east are becoming flushed with the new daylight.

Their conversation has aroused the two warrior escorts in Marheyo's hut and they are standing just outside the opening blinking at Melvill and Toby.

"My apologies," says Melvill. "Didn't mean to wake you."

Melvill and Toby return inside to their sleeping mats. There is nothing to do until the Typee family arises and prepares breakfast. Nothing to do but lie on the uncomfortable mat feeling the pulse-pain in his leg and thinking the terrible thoughts about Toby's departure.

three

~

Morning is the same except for the secret knowledge that Toby is leaving. Melvill can barely eat his breakfast. Toby's eating is slow and deliberate, as if it is an unpleasant task which must be accomplished. When the bowls and cups are cleared away, Marheyo begins shooing everyone but Melvill out of the hut. Melvill does not want to be occupied, even with Fayaway, when Toby leaves. He begins to protest but Toby stops him, "Just go along, old fellow. Let's not arouse suspicion more than is necessary."

So Melvill goes to his mat wondering if Toby is initiating his rescue or his lonely exile. On his way out of the hut Toby takes a bunch of bananas from the wall. No one seems to notice or care. Melvill is too nervous to lie still. He sits up and looks toward the opening where Toby has vanished. He thinks for a moment he can make the journey and wants to call out to Toby to wait. But Melvill knows it is a ludicrous thought. Marheyo, who has been fussing with bowls not used at breakfast, motions for Melvill to lie back and says something about Fayaway.

Melvill hesitates then reclines as ordered. He listens closely for the sounds of commotion but everything seems normal: another day for the Typees. He continues to listen intently, straining so hard he thinks perhaps he might hear a sail flapping on the windy sea. Nothing.

In a moment Fayaway is there with the tortoise-shell bowl and her glittering eyes. She greets him warmly and familiarly—

as she might her favorite pet that she has come to groom. Melvill slides down his pant leg and exposes his healing limb. He finds it hard to believe that Fayaway's primitive treatments are the cause of his improvement; but there is no question his leg is getting better.

Today Fayaway's hands are just as soothing and her face as beautiful and her slender brown body just as alluring but Melvill does not have to fight the waves of arousal. He is too distracted by the idea of being without Toby—of being abandoned here in this alien cannibal world. Melvill continually glances to the hut's entryway.

When Fayaway is finished, Melvill helps himself up with the crutch. He goes outside in only his shirt and underbreeches. Slowly, barefoot, he makes his way toward the bathing pool. Fayaway follows him, perhaps afraid he will fall. Korykory does not come for him as usual.

The streamwater is cool. Near Melvill a boy and girl splash in the pool, frolicking more than bathing. Fayaway waits on the bank by his crutch and clothes. Melvill shuts his eyes and wonders what has become of Toby. He reclines his head and water fills his ears, making him hear the sea. When he looks up again, Korykory and Marheyo are there talking to Fayaway, who appears concerned and puzzled.

Melvill calls out, "What is it? What are you saying?"

Marheyo blurts out something "taboo" and "Toby" and "wai" (water, Melvill has learned) and "kiki," then something "Happar." The old man is angry.

Melvill's heart is pounding. He is agitated because he understands so little. Toby is gone and he has taken water and food, it seems. But what about the Happars? "Is Toby all right?"

Marheyo shakes his head, apparently also frustrated with the language barrier, and turns away. He says something more to Korykory and Fayaway and the two rush in the direction of the grove, where Toby would have begun his trek. Marheyo walks wearily away. And Melvill is left alone except for the boy and girl, who are oblivious beyond their own carefree play.

Melvill gets out of the pool and into his breeches. He methodically returns to Marheyo's hut. Are the Typees looking at him differently, their dark faces a mixture of contempt and fear? And where have Korykory and Fayaway gone? To find Toby?

Inside Marheyo's hut the old man and his wife are involved in a serious discussion. They seem to take no notice of Melvill, exhausted in spite of the rush of anxiety he still feels. He leans on his crutch just inside the hut's opening. In a while they end their conversation and Marheyo leaves the hut, rushing in his old man's way; he neither looks at nor speaks to Melvill as he passes. Meanwhile Tinor goes to the corner where the bowls of food are kept. She begins the work of mixing a powder into the boacho then into the poeepoee.

Uncomfortable with the silence, Melvill says, "We have done nothing wrong. We cannot stay here forever. That was never our intention." Tinor does not look up from her mixing. "Toby—"

Tinor twists to him snakelike: "Taboo! Taboo!" She points her long finger at him; it is crooked with rheumatism.

"All right, old witch, his name is taboo. But he is only trying to secure better treatment for my leg and a means of departure."

Tinor says more, including something about the Happars. She punctuates her remark with a forced bit of laughter but Melvill is surprised to see a tear slip down her leathery brown cheek. He dresses himself.

In a moment Marheyo is back with several palmetto leaves and a wad of twine. They begin pouring the boacho and poeepoee, which now have a gelatinous consistency, into the long narrow leaves. Marheyo skillfully folds and rolls and ties the leaves into tight tubes. Melvill watches mutely and counts as they prepare twenty-eight leaf tubes. They are preparing for a famine, speculates Melvill, brought on by Toby's taboo departure. Poor simple people.

Marheyo leaves with a basket filled with the leaf tubes. Melvill decides to follow him in spite of the pain in his leg, and the growing irritation under his right arm from the roughly fashioned crutch. He suspects that Marheyo will forbid him to follow but the rigid old man says nothing as he heads toward the grove. Melvill cannot keep up so by the time Marheyo enters the ring of trees he is thirty or forty paces behind. Melvill, sweating and nearly panting, watches and follows until Marheyo stops at a plot of sandy ground where several Typees are using ax-like tools to dig shallow holes. They are burying their leaf tubes inside sheets of tappa. Marheyo picks up a spare ax-tool and begins digging also.

"This isn't necessary," Melvill says to the whole group. "T— His departure will not initiate floods and famine. That is singularly ludicrous." None of the workers pay attention to his meaningless chatter. He might as well have been a macaw clucking in a tree. "Go on. Dig your holes. Bury your food like a pack of paranoid dogs." At least they are not burying me in the sand, he thinks suddenly.

Melvill turns away and wonders what to do next. He is so tired and upset he cannot think clearly. It is like his brain is on fire, his thoughts smoldering into smoke. He hobbles on his crutch back to Marheyo's hut. The atmosphere is charged with tension. The mat in front of the hut's entryway has been removed and someone, Tinor presumably, has poured water on the hard ground to make a small plot of mud. A symbol with wavy lines—water? the sea?—has been etched into the quickly drying earth. Perhaps it is his imagination but Melvill believes he can smell the ocean more distinctly than before; it has been only an occasional whisper on the hot wind.

Melvill speculates the symbol on the ground is to keep out bad luck, but does that apply to him as well? Not wanting to risk another chastisement from Tinor, he turns away and goes to a log by the small fire pit. The orange embers remind him first of his mother's kitchen stove, then of the hell stoves in the

Acushnet. Both now seem as distant as a dream.

Sitting on the log is making his bad leg go numb. He thinks of how long Toby has been gone—only an hour?—and wonders how much time will pass before Toby returns. Will I continue to count the minutes and days and weeks even after the point when Toby could reasonably be back, then possibly be back, then beyond possibility? Melvill imagines his life of waiting and counting. Eternally on duty in the crow's nest watching for a whale that never breaks the surface. Or he imagines himself a whaleman's wife that watches year upon year for an impossible sail to appear on the distant oceanic horizon. A watcher who goes mad with watching.

Time, which has had little meaning since they jumped ship, is totally lost to Melvill while he sits on the log—awash in forlornness. He is only remotely aware of the sun's climb toward its apex and the growing heat on his shoulders. Also, the movement of the villagers around him is sensed only in a primitive way. But suddenly their pace is frantic. Running, chattering. Melville rises with difficulty, almost falling before he can get his weight on his crutch. "What is it? What's happening?"

A woman passing whom Melvill does not know says *something Toby.*

Melvill hobbles after the flock as they hurry toward the grove. He begins to imagine the worst—to feel the guilt, desperation, fear. All there in the cavity of his gut. Before he can reach the trees encircling the grove the villagers are coming back. At the center now is Korykory carrying Toby's limp form. Toby's hand, hanging down like a ragdoll's, is bloodstained. A sleeve of his shirt is ripped. His neck and face are bloody too.

"Is he dead?" Melvill pleads for an answer. "Tell me, is he dead?"

Korykory speaks to Melvill as the group passes around him. Fayaway, whom Melvill has not noticed, holds him by the arm and helps him to try to keep pace. Korykory takes

Toby into Marheyo's hut; only Marheyo and then Fayaway and Melvill follow inside. Korykory places Toby on a mat then begins feeling his head and neck and shoulders. Melvill pushes past Marheyo and Tinor: "Please, is Toby alive?" Korykory responds without looking at Melvill but of course his words carry no meaning. Melvill drops to Toby's side and takes hold of his wrist but before he can find his friend's pulse Toby moans and rolls his head. "Thank God," whispers Melvill.

Fayaway is now kneeling at Toby's other side. She has a sponge and a bowl of water and begins cleansing his wounds, which seem primarily to be two lacerations, one above his left eye and the other on his right cheekbone.

Marheyo and Korykory urge Melvill to stand. They say something about Fayaway, perhaps that she should be left alone to finish tending to Toby's cuts. Outside the village is quiet. The crowd that accompanied Toby back to Marheyo's hut has dispersed. The old man and Korykory exchange a few words; then unexpectedly Marheyo jerks the crutch away from Melvill and at the same instant Korykory hoists him onto his strong back.

"What're you doing?" Melvill struggles lamely for a moment but Korykory is carrying him toward the grove while Marheyo follows with his crutch in hand. "To the Ti?"

Neither native responds.

Into the grove and down a path Melvill has not traveled before. It is shaded and quiet—not even the birds are calling. Then they come to a cluster of huts, much like the cluster where Marheyo's family lives, except these huts sit on the shore of a large pond, nearly a lake, Melvill thinks. There is another cluster of huts two hundred yards or more around the bend of the pond, and in between is a group of Typees. This is where Korykory and Marheyo are transporting him. When the group senses their arrival it parts instinctively. They are gathered around a stone slab on which lies a young warrior. Melvill recognizes him as one of Toby's escorts. Dead. There is a large puncture wound in his left ribcage, perhaps from a spear, which still leaks blood. Village girls, as young as seven or eight, are making a garland of white flowers across his body.

Melvill is let down from Korykory's back and Marheyo begins speaking to him, telling him a story it seems. Melvill understands the warrior's name, "Toonoo," and "Happar." Several times Marheyo touches his own side where Toonoo was pierced and says, "muckee moee," which Melvill assumes refers to death or being killed. Marheyo's tale also has "taboo" and "Toby."

"I understand," says Melvill. "This young man's death was caused by Toby—by his leaving or by his stepping foot into Happar territory. Or by both. I'm sorry, truly, but we cannot be imprisoned here because of your primeval customs."

Marheyo responds with something more, but *about* "Hermes," not *to him* precisely. The old man with tattooed vines growing along his arms like jungle ivy shakes his head in disgust or frustration. Korykory gestures to Melvill to climb on his back. The great distance to Toby and to the shelter of Marheyo's hut makes it necessary. However at this moment the thing Melvill desires the least is Typee charity, which only compounds his miserable guilt. Melvill takes his crutch from Marheyo and slides it into the back of his shirt like an arrow into its quiver; then climbs onto Korykory's avian inked back.

The whole Typee Valley is quiet still, yet the air is tinged with excitement and activity. In preparation for what? reflects Melvill as he is carried along. Not famine still? No, it is something else, something more. When they have passed through the grove and its outer ring of trees Korykory lets Melvill down. He must hobble from here, which is perfectly acceptable to Melvill, a relief really. He uses the crutch for the remainder; Korykory stays at his side, though to do so he must move slowly and awkwardly.

Inside Marheyo's hut Fayaway is still tending to Toby. Now she is sponging water into his mouth. He semiconsciously swallows the drops. A glob like brown mud covers the cut on Toby's head. The crude poultice has stopped the bleeding and Toby is not as pale.

Thank God, thinks Melvill: Toby will live—unless a Typee devil decides to exact some recompense for the death of Toonoo. Melvill sits by his friend and Fayaway hands him a cup of water. It is warm but delicious nonetheless. "Thank you, and thank you for caring for Toby."

Fayaway smiles slightly. At the recognition of Toby's name?

Melvill has a thousand questions—about the death of the warrior and what it means and why the Happars attacked Toby and if he was rescued by the Typees, about Toby's condition—but there is no one to ask.

While Toby sleeps they have a simple lunch in the hut: Tinor, Korykory, Fayaway and Melvill. Marheyo has not returned. Melvill feels he should not have an appetite—because of Toby's convalescence and in mourning Toonoo—but he is famished. The slightly unripe bananas and poeepoee only begin to satisfy him. He is thinking about going to a section of the grove where a tangerine-like fruit grows and surreptitiously eating his fill; however before he can commit to his plan there is a visitor to the hut, one of Toby's warrior escorts. He speaks quietly to Korykory. Melvill hears "Marheyo" and "Mehevi." He notices that Tinor and Fayaway have no interest in the conversation as if they already know its purpose. When the discussion is finished the young warrior departs. Korykory looks at Melvill but says nothing. He saves his breath though he wants to know what is happening.

After a few more minutes of sitting quietly by Toby while Tinor and Fayaway gather the dirty bowls and cups, the gnawing in his stomach makes him forget about Korykory's conversation. He gets up and starts to leave the hut. Korykory quickly blocks his way. He speaks ardently to Melvill putting his hands up urging him to wait.

"Look here, I simply want to go for a stretch. My leg is

stiffening." That much is true; he rubs his bad leg.

Korykory is insistent. He even tries using an English word: "*Pah-leez.*"

Melvill is wondering what to do when the young warrior appears again in the doorway. Korykory is greatly relieved. Now he wants Melvill to go outside. The remainder of Toby's escort is there, and they are standing around a long flat board which is secured at its corners to two sturdy poles. Korykory urges Melvill toward the board. "Yes, I can see it. What do you want me to do?" Korykory encourages him closer then goes past Melvill and sits in the center of the board. "I understand," says Melvill. "It's a litter." He nods to emphasize his recognition. Korykory jumps up and ushers Melvill to his seat. Melvill is reluctant but he has no desire to make another spectacle. When he is seated in the middle of the litter, the four young warriors hoist him up, first to arm's length, then to their shoulders; and they begin toward the grove.

Typees, especially children, stare at Melvill as he and his entourage pass—like some damn Oriental prince, he thinks. Beyond the grove they take a wide path which cuts directly toward the sea. Melvill believes he can smell its salt even though it is miles away and not within view. All he can see is the sandy path through the forest and to his left and back the purpleblue mountain tops. Now and then they encounter a native, who glances as he hurries along, either passing them or going the opposite way.

Eventually the path emerges from the forest and begins to climb uphill, up out of the Typee Valley. Melvill thinks about how the warriors carrying him must be laboring now. Melvill glances behind at Korykory, faithfully keeping his crutch. On either side of the path, which is less sandy here and more grayblack volcanic dirt, the grasscovered hills are spotted with colorful wildflowers: orange starshape bursts, red and yellow and blue puffs like sea anemones. Finally the path crests and instantly declines a hundred yards to a wide plain where wind moves across the grass in waves.

The breeze is so fresh Melvill breathes it deeply, even greedily. The air is one thing he loves about the ocean. The sea air is freedom . . . and life unevolved, hence uncompromised by the modern world. Perhaps that is why he despises the cooking blubber so—the stench overpowers the ocean's natural scent, corrupting the sea air for miles. The sky too, here, is the ocean's: steely and powerful, a presence itself, a mighty dome arching above the mighty sea.

Melvill sees a shack, a good old New England shack, made of boards instead of indigenous bamboo. The shack is leaning in toward the path and its boards are sunbleached gray. It must have been a white man's hand that constructed it—but how many years before?

As they travel along the level grade, the sea is revealed to Melvill. It is spread out blue, like an emperor's silk gown. The natives quickly but gently maneuver Melvill's litter to the ground near the shack before breaking formation to catch their breath, each in his own way, bending at the waist or dropping to his knees or walking about with his hands on his hips. They remind Melvill of Greek messengers winded after their long run to Marathon. Korykory, not winded at all, helps Melvill up then hands him his crutch.

Melvill is enchanted by the sight of the ocean. It seems as unreal as a painting, even though it moves and rushes against the whitesand beach. He is thinking about the image when Typees begin to emerge from the shack. He recognizes one as Mehevi. The cannibal chief is not smiling as he has been quick to do in the Ti. Another Typee, also heavily decorated like Mehevi, is fiercer looking and has only one eye. The empty socket, which is in shadow because of the overhead sun, draws Melvill's attention. He forces himself to look into the native's good eye, where he finds disdain, as if Melvill is a diseased animal whose pitiful life should be stamped out. A broad circle has been tattooed around the solitary brown orb, making it a bull's-eye, as if the cannibal is daring some enemy to blind him completely.

Melvill wonders at the hierarchy of this group. Are these other Typees, eight in number, Mehevi's cabinet of advisers? Or is the cannibal nation run more by committee, of which Mehevi is the chairman, and these other Typees are simply lesser chieftains, one of whom will one day take over the committee— by mutual agreement or by force? From his demeanor, the single-eyed Typee is perhaps a sort of captain of the guard.

Mehevi steps close enough to Melvill to touch him and begins speaking to him in low serious tones, something about the Happars again and "muckee moee," that ominous phrase that holds death in it. Then Mehevi takes Melvill by the arm which is not gripping the crutch and leads him to the graybleached shack. It has no door, and inside Melvill is surprised to find an ancient Typee warrior, an old old man on a mat on the shack's sandy dirt floor. The ancient one's eyes are staring vacantly out the doorway, perhaps at the ocean-like sky.

Also inside the shack is a collection of firearms, which seem to be why Mehevi has brought him here. Some of the pieces appear to be fairly contemporary but poorly maintained. Others, muskets and even a brace of blunderbusses, are very old—mid-eighteenth century, Melvill speculates—and they are broken and rusted. There is even a fowling piece with a queen-anne stock like the one Melvill pawned in New York City before his first experience at sea as a deckhand on the Liverpool-bound *St. Lawrence*. In the corner of the shack several small kegs of shot and powder are piled, as are boxes of ammunition in various calibers.

Mehevi seems to be telling Melvill about the weapons.

Melvill nods, though he barely understands. "How in the world did you come by all these?" But Melvill can imagine how—some bartered for perhaps, others pried from the hands of their dead enemies.

Meanwhile Mehevi continues to talk about the weapons. He

pantomimes shooting, even the recoil. Mehevi unexpectedly takes hold of Melvill's hands, says a few last words and smiles, squeezing his hands for emphasis.

Melvill believes he understands. "You want me to get these weapons in working order. But not all white men are gunsmiths; I certainly am not." He recalls the corpse of the young warrior, his ribs leaking blood onto the stone slab, the garland of white flowers strung by the children. "I'll see what I can do—no promises however." Melvill nods exaggeratedly: "Yes, I'll see what I can do."

Mehevi, pleased, leaves the shack and speaks to his comrades. He seems to be reassuring them.

Melvill stands fixed for a few moments. "What do you see, old man?" he says to the entranced warrior but of course there is no response. He begins his work by first examining each of the guns and separating out the ones which are obviously in need of specialized repair. The remainder—eight fairly contemporary pieces, three European-made and five American-, including a good pair of flintlock Kentucky rifles and two single-shot flintlock pistols—appear as though a thorough cleaning may make them serviceable. He decides the prize piece though is a Wheeler revolving cylinder flintlock that can be fired seven times before reloading. His mind is already collecting locally available items which might be used for the task of servicing the weapons when he finds a wooden box among the piles of casks and crates that contains various types of cloth, bottles of oil, a ram rod, plus an assortment of files and other fine tools, screws and springs.

"The fates continue to watch over me," Melvill says to his silent companion.

For some time he sits on a crate and works at the guns, cleaning and oiling, checking their hammers and triggers, their breech and firing mechanisms, the straightness of their barrels, that their muzzles are clear, and making what few minor repairs he feels capable of—all that he knows to do. After, he sorts shot and powder and cartridges, matching each to the appropriate firearm. For all this time none of the Typees have looked in on him; and the old warrior in the shack has made no sound, virtually no movement. His remaining purpose in life seems to be as guardian of this cache of mysterious weaponry.

Melvill hobbles out into the bright day and speaks to Mehevi, who with the other Typees has been resting in a shaded area on the grassy hillock. "Finished," he says, "to the best of my knowledge. But I'm not testing them. I'll leave your boys the brunt of burst barrels."

Mehevi smiles at Melvill's words then follows him into the shack. Melvill points out which ammunition to use with which gun. He is about to demonstrate to Mehevi how to load them when the chief excitedly takes hold of the unloaded Wheeler and it is clear he has some familiarity with its use. The one-eyed Typee also enters the shack. He looks as stern and disgusted as before. Then Korykory is there to lead Melvill back to the litter.

"Come, footmen," says Melvill, "back to the palace." He realizes his hunger and exhaustion as he sits on the flat board. Korykory, as if by telepathy, hands him three small bananas in exchange for his crutch. Before peeling one Melvill breathes the saltfresh air deeply for a last time.

It is a long way back. When they reach the Ti the natives set Melvill down, then they rush off toward the mountains with another group of young warriors.

As Korykory helps Melvill to stand, he says, "Is there to be war then?"

Korykory makes no attempt to respond other than to hand Melvill his crutch, and they slowly complete the journey to Marheyo's hut. By the sun Melvill guesses it is three or four in the afternoon. Late for warring, he thinks. Inside the hut Toby is conscious. "Old fellow," he says weakly.

Melvill sits beside him on the floor. "Glad to have you back with us, Lazarus." He squeezes Toby's forearm.

"What's happening?"

"I'm not certain but I believe the Typees and Happars are going to battle."

"Because of me?"

Melvill hesitates. "That appears to have triggered it—but these islanders have a hair trigger. Their superstitions are so thick it takes very little to upset them."

Melvill lies back and soon dozes next to Toby. It seems a very short time before the report of a distant gunshot startles him. He sits up. He and Toby are alone. There is another shot. And another. Melvill looks at Toby, who is awake but silent. Melvill slowly goes to the hut's opening. It is nearing sunset. The air seems to retain the glow of daylight even though the sun has descended from view. Melvill steps outdoors and there are fires in the Ti grove. Two more gunshots in immediate succession.

Toby joins Melvill outdoors.

"Should you be up?"

"Probably not." Toby steadies himself by holding Melvill's arm. "But I must know what is happening."

Melvill retrieves his crutch and they make their way toward the grove. When they reach the ring of trees the orange firelight has overtaken the daylight in dominance. Trying to remain out of view they enter the grove behind the Ti and cautiously stay near its side wall until they achieve a view of the grove's interior. There are several small fires. The natives are gathered near the center of the grove where a small bamboo scaffold has been erected. Melvill speculates it is seven or eight feet high. It is difficult to see in the strange light but there appears to be a white bundle on the top of the scaffold. Melvill is reminded of the pile of bedding he has seen at home on washday since before he can recall.

Melvill is about to whisper to Toby, to ask what he thinks is happening, when the scaffold is ignited. Flames burst up nearly in an explosion. The wood must have been treated with some combustible agent. The intense fire illuminates the encircling crowd of Typees, who begin a low chant.

"What's queer about that gathering?" says Toby then answers himself: "It's all women and children and old men."

Melvill watches as the firetongues leap at the white bundle and it begins to smoke. The form of the bundle is clearer now and Melvill instantly understands: it is Toonoo's funeral pyre. Melvill wants to tell Toby but at the moment it is too much to explain.

"Where are the men, the warriors?" says Toby. "Still fighting?"

Melvill has no response. He searches the crowd for Fayaway. It is a pool of brown flesh and long black hair, all the bodies rouged by firelight, and he recognizes no one.

A shadow emerges from the path that leads to the mountains, the one that Toby traveled that morning. Several Typees break away from the chanting group to speak with the new arrival, who Melvill can see is a young man—very young, no more than sixteen probably. After a short exchange the young man turns and runs toward another path, the one that leads to the place where Marheyo buried food. The firelight glows then fades on the adolescent's back as he rushes away, until he is invisible in the forest's blackness.

Melvill whispers, "I believe I know where he is going."

Careful to avoid the ring of light they methodically make their way to the path not quite halfway around the grove. When they are on the path and leaving the grove behind Melvill says, "How are you feeling?"

"Fair. My head is aching some, but all right otherwise. You?"

"The leg is much improved. The crutch is almost unnecessary." Melvill realizes the irony: the primary justification for Toby's leaving was to obtain medical care for his leg, and now it seems nearly healed.

The path is dark but Melvill's eyes have adjusted. He thinks of the suffocating darkness in the hold of the *Acushnet*: the low ceiling closing in like the top of a cage, the stench of rot. And the movement underfoot, the whaleship always moving, a predatory shark forever on the hunt for victims, an unslakable thirst to turn life into death. He sees the bluegray ocean burst into that obscene orange color when it is suddenly filled with animal blood. Death is not black; it is orange, that cloud of rust in the sea.

Melvill forces the hunting thoughts to cease. He must be alert. They do not want to encounter a party of Typees still swooning with bloodlust. After a short time they reach the small clearing where Marheyo and others had buried food. It seems deserted. Only a warm breeze. And a dazzling night sky. Melvill instantly recognizes the constellation Orion. A halfmoon is etched above a stand of trees. Melvill notices that the trees are strangely illuminated, black against an artificial light.

"This way," says Melvill, leading Toby over the plot of ground where the poeepoee and boacho leaftubes are buried. His crutch digs into the soft earth. They discover that the stand of trees is at the edge of a ravine, and in the ravine all the Typee men are gathered around a circle of fires. For such a large gathering—two hundred? three?—they are oddly quiet; the only sounds are their random movements about the fires. Melvill estimates the circle is thirty to forty yards in diameter.

Like the Typees, Melvill and Toby are completely silent as they watch. Melvill is startled by a thump . . . then another—like the beating of a drum, a slow steady rhythm. It takes a moment to find its source: it is a young man—possibly the adolescent Toby and he followed to this place—and he is striking a hollow log with a short wooden club. Melvill realizes the movement of the Typees is no longer random. They are taking up very particular positions around the fires. One Typee seems to be the attendant of a fire and behind him a line forms, from youngest (strongest?) to most senior. Melvill recalls that the old old men are back in the Ti grove.

The Feast

In a moment young men come from Melvill's left—from an area out of view—and they are carrying baskets with long sticks protruding from them. The baskets resemble large exotic insects, upended, in the odd light from the fires. The basketbearers take up positions to the immediate right of each fire attendant. They all remain quiet, immobile, like the ancient warrior in the gun shack. Melvill imagines the Typee is still there in the dark keeping his silent vigil.

When all are in place the rhythmic beating on the log ceases for a moment—skipping one . . . two beats—then resumes. There is movement from the left. It is a man wearing a hood and cape of feathers. Melvill assumes them to be parrot feathers. When the man enters the circle of fires and stops at the center Melvill realizes it is Mehevi. The king is to officiate, he thinks. Mehevi slowly turns so that he eventually faces all the Typees in line at the fires. His arms are at his sides hidden by the cloak of feathers. As he completes the circle he lifts an arm—a wing— to others out of view. The natives around the fires keep their attention fixed; they do not turn to watch the action.

Melvill is both repelled and spellbound by what he sees next. Two Typees carry long poles into the circle and mounted on each is a head. The eyes and mouths are open, as if screaming. The poles glisten with blood in the firelight. They are planted in the ground on either side of Mehevi. They go into the earth so deeply and so easily the holes must have been made in advance.

Mehevi lifts his wings and speaks to the assemblage: a proclamation? a prayer? He finishes shortly and each fire attendant removes a stick from the basket. Food is skewered on the end of the stick—and Melvill knows that it is human meat, the flesh of these two Happars. Perhaps in the mountainous Happar region they are dining on a pair of fallen Typees at this same moment, a barbaric equilibrium at work in the universe.

Except there is no sense of barbarism in their behavior, no jeering at the dead Happars. There is a solemnity to the ritual, almost a holiness, like they are paying homage to the slain warriors.

There is popping in the fires as droplets of fat and blood fall into the flames. The aroma that is beginning to drift from the ravine is like nothing Melvill has ever smelled: strong but slightly sweet. He knows he will never forget the scent. His mouth is watering—an animal response to the smell of food—and it sickens him. He glances at Toby to check his reaction but it is too dark along the rim of the ravine. He knows he cannot watch the cannibals consume their meat.

He whispers to Toby, "I'm going back," as he turns away from the ancient spectacle.

Toby is there with him as he slowly crosses the clearing, his leg stiff from standing in one place for so long. They do not speak. Their silence is all that is keeping the world real. Melvill feels that he is traversing the brink of some nightmarish fiction, a treacherous precipice above a world he is incapable of comprehending, a place where his ignorance would be eternal. He senses he may spend the rest of his days attempting to grasp this new place in which he finds himself . . . or has lost himself.

No one sees them as they retrace their path; perhaps they are invisible now, like the spirits of the fallen warriors whose presence lingers in the blackjungled world.

In Marheyo's hut Melvill curls into his space. It is a terrible night between the realms of consciousness and unconsciousness, fighting the urge to sleep for fear of dreaming, but dreaming off and on nevertheless. The cannibal ritual and recollections from the whaler mix and fuse. The Typees are gathered for their terrible feast on the goreslick deck of the *Acushnet*; Melvill and Toby stare down from the rigging. Then it is their shipmates who are lining up for the meat in the ravine. Fat Captain Pease, tattooed so completely only his eyes are untouched by the needle, is orchestrating the meal from the circle of fires, his arms become great taloned wings. . . .

four

~~~

Will they appear different? How can they not? And Fayaway too—will the stain of blood be upon her as well? Melvill realizes he had stopped thinking of the Typees as cannibals sometime before. They were simply strange islanders. The menace has returned: the possibility of cruel death followed by the unthinkable horror. But that is precisely it. It is thinkable now. Cannibalism is real—like the whales who break water, sudden islands in the sea, like the ancient green continent of Europe, like your father's funeral, like your mother's weeping at it. Like Christianity? Like a heaven and a hell?

Marheyo and the others had returned in the night, the smell of woodsmoke clinging in the dark. It was late: their cannibal rituals had persisted past the midnight hour. When Melvill looks at Marheyo in faintest light of day, the old man awake bumping around the hut, he expects to see the reddish brown stain on his face. At first, still feigning sleep, he believes he does see the mark of the feast; but it is only shadows in the gloomy hut. The rest of the natives in the hut are snoring peacefully, exhausted no doubt from their long night.

Marheyo steps out into the early day. Melvill checks Toby and he too seems to be sleeping. For a moment he wonders about his friend's dreaming, was it as bizarre as his own? Melvill, as quietly as he is able with his stiff leg and his crutch, follows Marheyo out of the hut. The sky is graywhite for lack of sunlight.

The old man is out of view. Melvill assumes he is headed for the reeds near the stream to relieve himself. That is the direction Melvill heads, his crutch swinging along beside him. But Marheyo is not at the reed patch; no one is. His next guess is the Ti grove and in a few minutes he finds Marheyo there cleaning up the remains of Toonoo's funeral, the charred wood and ashes. Three other old men are assisting. Unlike the previous night, Melvill does not try to stay hidden. He rests on a log in front of the Ti as the natives scoop the ashes onto a large swath of cloth, longer and wider than a bedsheet—perhaps a twin to the one in which Toonoo was wrapped at his funeral. When the evidence is all gathered they meticulously fold the cloth until the four corners are brought into a bundle. Then one of the old men takes it and begins down the sea path. Marheyo and the others rake at the sandy ground with long sticks until all indications of the funeral pyre are erased.

Marheyo comes to Melvill on the log and says something about breakfast, "kiki," and they return to his hut. Everyone is awake and Tinor is preparing the meal.

Toby looks tired still.

"How was your sleep?" Melvill asks.

"Dreadful, truly."

Melvill thinks vaguely of his own dreams but the events that inspired them are already beginning to mutate—too unreal, or surreal, for his mind to hold onto the exact details.

After their simple breakfast Marheyo clears everyone from the hut except Melvill. Fayaway is coming. Melvill's pulse quickens at the thought of her. Fayaway's sexual appeal has always been great but now that she is truly part of a cannibal tribe her persona is even more powerful. Along with the beauty, the long firm lines of her juvenile body, there is an element of danger: leanjungled and predatory.

Melvill's mind is beginning to conjure all kinds of images of Fayaway when she arrives at the hut, the sound of Marheyo greeting her outside. Melvill looks up anticipating the face of his fancy and is somewhat surprised, disappointed even, to see sweetlooking Fayaway smiling at him, as docile as any New England schoolgirl. In fact today she is wearing a piece of tappa on her shoulders tied at the neck so that it obscures her breasts. Melvill has only seen older Typee women who are working in the sun cover themselves in this way, their breasts swaying like bags of grain under the loose cloth.

She places the tortoise-shell bowl on the floor as Melvill bares his leg. Before coating her hands Fayaway inspects the leg, kneading its flesh. She comments on the "*league*" and uses a Typee word that Melvill recognizes: "arva," strong.

"Yes, regaining some of its use has strengthened the limb."

She smiles and says "arva" again. Then Fayaway dips her hands into the gelatinous mixture, coating them thoroughly, and she begins massaging Melvill's toes and foot.

Melvill tries to distract himself by thinking about the battle with the Happars. Is that it? A brief jungle skirmish and a few fallen warriors—and the conflict is resolved? What a delicate balance the enemies have achieved, such a small misstep can throw them at each other. Yet they do not seem intent on genocide. Perhaps they have an instinctive understanding of the greater dangers from without: the Europeans and Americans who will eventually encroach upon them to extinction. He thinks of the native inhabitants of his own country and their steadily being driven west and being diminished every step of the long slow journey. The ointment's afterheat is engulfing his foot and ankle.

Fayaway's touch explores the skull-like structure of his knee. She always lingers for a moment at the small scar on the skin holding the patella, the result of bounding over an ancient fence and cutting himself on a nail. The torn pant leg and the blood soaking through are still vivid boyhood memories. Fayaway, perhaps enveloped in her own reverie, moves above the knee to the thigh. Her fingers seem to tug marionette strings to his organ, which twitches to her delicate manipulations, a supple dance partner. His scrotum swells with the vitality of swimming life.

Impulsively Melvill reaches up and unties the tappa shroud around Fayaway's shoulders and it falls away. He allows himself a moment's glance at her lovely breasts; and even in that brief instant he can see her nipples rising. Hungry, consumed, he looks into her eyes, fresh and ancient at the same moment. Her hands are on his thigh but her fingers are motionless. Melvill realizes he is salivating, like at the cannibal's feast.

There is something in Fayaway's eyes but he cannot interpret it. Even her emotions are transmitted in this alien island vernacular. Melvill begins to summon words; however his brain is slow traveling from the primeval to the modern day. Fayaway diverts her eyes, picks up the white cloth and bowl, and rushes from the hut.

Melvill stares at the dark thatched ceiling. Miserable with longing and self-reproach. Gorged with emptiness. He feels as though everything is falling asunder: events are beyond his control yet his actions affect them. It is a familiar feeling— his father's death, the family business faltering, the trip west to Illinois to try his hand at farming, life aboard the *Acushnet*, and now this nightmarish place, where only some mystical force prevents his murder.

Melvill rises and uses his crutch to walk toward the bathing pool. His pant leg sticks in the half-applied ointment. Are the Typees staring at him? Do they know of his indiscretion? The pace of the villagers seems slowed as if the recent events have sapped their energies. Melvill feels weakened too. At the edge of the pool he disrobes completely then sinks into the cool water letting himself drop down like an iron ball. Down until his toes feel the sand and pebbles, then his legs and buttocks. There he sits submerged, the sharper stones digging into his flesh giving him pain and a kind of pleasure. The heat from the jungle ointment on his leg dissipating in the mountainfed stream, the current running cold as Allegheny snow on the bottom. The water fills his ears, shutting out a world beyond his comprehension anyway.

Melvill is naked and alone in the womb of the stream.

five

～～～

The rectangle of the hut's opening is still the black of pure night. He is surprised that his mind is not picking over the Typees' battle nor their cannibal banquet but of an incident on the *Acushnet* instead. Below deck hunting for a keg of pennynails the manifest says is in store. The oil lamp burns out just as Melvill hears movement outside the door; then its opening to blackness and invisible Melvill within. He smells Taggart, the chiefmate, his odd Calcutta scent he puts on from a bottle. A voice begins, another's, but Taggart silences him: "Hush girlie, it can be bad for ya." The door shutting, not loudly like Melvill anticipates, quiet, not even the old seabitten hinges squeaking, as if they too are fearful of Taggart, strange and meanspirited as a basketed cobra. Then there's the rustling of clothing in the dark, Taggart's heavy ornate beltbuckle, Spanish silver, hitting the floor with a thump. Then in a moment the suckling sounds, Melvill visualizing a grotesque infant at its mother's misshapen tit. And Taggart, that sound of animal satisfaction. Melvill breathing shallow and fast hoping that only his own ears can hear his respiration. He knows the other person is young Jones form New York City, knows it by means of a sense he cannot name. Minutes click by in the dark hold. Rats move somewhere among the crates and kegs, their claws tapping along like blindmen's sticks. Blindmen at home in the deepest black. Finally Taggart's silent eruption. All movement stops for a long moment, save the perpetual sway of the ship, the swing of the dark lamp on its nail, before the rustling of clothing again. "You be quiet as a dead man. You hear my words girlie: quiet as a dead man." When Taggart leaves first, Melvill wants to say something to Jones but adequate words will not form. He stays invisible until Jones too is gone, no doubt heavy and lost. In the middle of the greengray ocean.

six

~~~~~~~

Melvill watches surreptitiously as Marheyo prepares for the new day. The old warrior stretches, a joint pops then another. He goes to the hut's opening and peers into the gathering light. He shuffles back inside to speak some quiet words to Tinor, who is still lying on the floor under a sheet of tappa; she returns his quiet words. Marheyo takes a long walking stick which has not moved from its place on the wall since Melvill and Toby's arrival. It appears fashioned from a gnarled limb of a strong tree. Then he takes two bananas from a bunch hanging in the corner and he leaves the hut.

Melvill wants to know where he is going but he pretends to sleep for a while longer and does doze a bit. It is Toby's getting up which fully rouses him. "Wake yourself, old fellow, something's happening."

Melvill sits upright and sees that Tinor and Korykory are fillings baskets with bowls and pots of food. Tinor turns to them and says something about water, "wai," and motions outside. "Come on," says Toby, "I believe she wants us to perform our morning duties." He helps Melvill stand and hands him the crutch. Toby no longer has his warrior escort—perhaps the Typees have decided they are unnecessary or ineffective.

The day is already hot. Melvill squints back at the mountains, where the white sun has fully cleared the peaks.

They return from the stream to find Tinor and Korykory and Fayaway outside the hut holding baskets of food and drink.

They all set off for the Ti grove. Through pantomime Toby offers to carry Fayaway's basket but she declines with a smile. Tinor however passes her basket to Toby, who accepts it after a moment's hesitation.

Melvill smiles. "Always the gentleman."

In the quiet grove they take the path which leads to the bamboo shrines. The jungle is still dark and cool, the overhead flora blocking the early rays of the sun. Unseen birds calling wildly break the jungle's weighty silence. Melvill wonders what they are all doing. They appear to be en route to a picnic breakfast, which is queer itself, but there is a seriousness surrounding the activity. They walk slowly and deliberately, almost ceremoniously. Melvill, with his crutch and his sore leg, has no trouble keeping their pace—he recalls walking to Sunday worship with his family as a boy. He does not bother asking for Toby's assessment. He could only respond with his own pure conjecture, and breaking the silence seems disrespectful.

Melvill observes each warrior shrine closely as they pass, each in a different phase of dilapidation, each with a stone totem guarding its black interior, each seeming to harbor the ghost of the departed warrior and the unleashed echoes of his battle stories. Bloody, glorious and horrible. The jungle path is more solemn than a graveyard.

They reach Marheyo's newly constructed shrine, and the old man is there to greet them. He has gotten a ceremonial cloak of feathers; he holds the gnarled stick. Marheyo greets each one by name: Korykory, Tinor, Fayaway, Toby, Hermes. It strikes Melvill how different the wood of Marheyo's shrine is from the others they have passed: dark and rich in color, not time- and weatherbleached. How ancient must some of the shrines be?

Tinor and Fayaway begin laying out the meal picnicstyle on the ground. When preparations are finished they sit at the edges of the tappa sheet. Melvill expects Marheyo to join them but he remains standing, pride painting his leathery face. The food is passed and Marheyo begins speaking. Even though he does not understand the words, Melvill feels that he should refrain from eating until Marheyo is finished—it may be some sort of benediction—but the Typees start to their meal. They eat and react nonverbally to Marheyo, following every word.

Melvill gets the impression he is recounting some history, perhaps his personal history. At times Marheyo acts out the story, thrusting as if he holds a spear instead of the gnarled aegis, later lifting some heavy object above his head. The story goes on and on. Instead of speaking to his audience Marheyo seems to have achieved a kind of trance. He is saying the words like they are part of a scripted prayer, but with full animation, not the monotone sermon of a Protestant minister. More like a bard reciting a Homeric hymn, thinks Melvill. Marheyo paddles through an evoked sea. The vines tattooed on his arms are like veins popping.

One by one they finish eating but the oration continues. Every so often the Typees smile at some detail in Marheyo's story. Melvill avoids making eye contact with Toby because no doubt they would exchange some glance—confused, frustrated, bemused—and Melvill does not want to show disrespect.

Melvill's mind is wandering when he hears "Toby bwa Hermes . . ." as Marheyo must have come to their part of his story. Shortly there is talk of Toonoo and again the Happars. The Typees' age-old enemies are an integral component of Marheyo's personal narrative, almost as if there would be no meaning to Marheyo's life, nor any Typee's, if not for their cannibal brethren. Their Cain-and-Abel brethren. Melvill wonders about Mexico and if that country will become like the Happars to the United States, an embittered enemy perched on its border.

Finally Marheyo finishes, and he wavers slightly, perhaps exhausted and relieved from the burden of his tale. Melvill thinks of the mixture of exhaustion and elation after sexual intercourse, rid temporarily of the burden of desire. The old man stares straight with an odd look of pride washing over his face while his family jabbers to him. Melvill imagines "Well done! Bravo! Well said!" The adoration continues for a prolonged time—until three Typees emerge from the path, two men and a woman, naked of course except for their white cloths, blue tattoos, and shells and feathers. Marheyo greets them, tears gathering in his ancient eyes. Meanwhile Tinor and Fayaway begin picking up the mess. Korykory rises and stands near his father. He too wears his pride like ceremonial garb.

Melvill and Toby also stand. They try to assist Tinor and Fayaway but there appears to be no need. They go to the nearby log.

"This must be some sort of gala opening," says Toby quietly.

"Yes, or a visitation, with the dear one present in both body and spirit." Other Typees are arriving as Melvill speaks.

Tinor and Fayaway have placed the baskets, now filled with the dirty bowls and cups and the soiled tappa, out of the way in some tall grass; they too stand next to the bamboo shrine but clearly apart from Marheyo and Korykory.

Melvill expects the visitors to shake hands with Marheyo. Instead they take hold of each other's wrists and stay locked that way while they talk a moment, all smiles and warmth on this hot tropical day. Then the visitors move on to Korykory, then Tinor and Fayaway, but only holding wrists with Marheyo. Melvill recalls hearing that Roman officers greeted their enemies in this way to begin discussing terms of surrender or truce: taking each other by the wrist to assure that neither was concealing a weapon. Melvill thinks that this Typee custom must have evolved from some other reasoning; he thinks of the pulse tapping and the tender skin at the wrist.

The exchanges between Marheyo and his visitors are brief—and meaningless to Melvill and Toby, who suggests that they return to the Ti for a smoke.

"Perhaps it would be uncouth to leave," says Melvill.

"No one will even notice us missing. We may as well be trees rooted here in the forest." It seems Toby is correct: old

Tinor and Fayaway are smiling and chatting as the visitors move through the line. They are coming from both directions on the path now but arranging themselves to speak with Marheyo first.

"You are probably right." Melvill tightens his grip on his crutch.

They leave the place quietly. For a moment Melvill tries to make eye contact with Fayaway but she is rapt in conversation. Without speaking they make their way toward the Ti, slowly at first because of Melvill's stiff leg, until the exercise loosens it somewhat. At the Ti Toby helps Melvill ascend to the stone portico. Inside the smoky Ti they find very few Typees—only old men who are closer to being dead than living. Soon they are sitting smoking; and Melvill, the tobacco smoke warm in his throat, realizes he feels at ease here, among the aged Typees and the severed heads of their enemies.

seven

~~~~~~~~~

Awake, Melvill reaches for his crutch. The hut is empty except for Tinor, who is preparing breakfast. Hungry, Melvill involuntarily thinks of a beefsteak and fried eggs, and flatcakes with maple syrup. Since the morning of Marheyo's ceremony life among the Typees has returned to its normal routine. Melvill counts the days: three mornings since the ceremony, or has it been four? It is easy to lose track but he is determined not to allow the time to melt away, like tallow, until it is a seamless indeterminate puddle.

He is outside when he realizes his leg no longer ails him. He takes a few cautious steps without supporting his weight on the crutch. There is the vaguest hint of stiffness at the hip joint— otherwise his limb is completely flexible and free of pain. He walks about taking giant strides. He hops. He skips.

"What's going on?" Toby has returned unnoticed.

"My leg, Tobias, it is cured—completely cured!" Melvill, holding the crutch in the air, dances a clumsy jig to illustrate.

"It doesn't pain you in the least?"

"No. There is a trace of rigidity here," says Melvill touching his hip, "but even that seems to be fading."

Marheyo and Korykory have also returned; they appear astonished.

"I am quite all better," Melvill says to the islanders, who are standing staring. "I must go; I must explore. Being free of the pain is so liberating." He sets off for the Ti grove, the crutch still in hand but not using it.

Toby trails after him: "Yes, but you mustn't overdo it—we don't want a relapse."

Almost at a run Melvill hears his friend's advice but ignores it. Melvill is amazed at how close the Ti seems to be at this pace. Reaching it before has been so laborious. The world has suddenly shrunk. The Hawaiian Islands feel within swimming distance. The sky is bright on this new day and the air fresh, like from the snowpeaked Alleghenys or the Atlantic, where glaciers float as if phantoms in the icy waters.

At the Ti grove Melvill studies the network of paths, feeling dazed and a little drunk. He says to Toby, who has caught up, "I must go but I can't decide where. You decide."

"I think you should stop and rest a moment, and make certain your leg is truly shipshape." Korykory is there too—dispatched to contain the lunatic.

"Sound advice no doubt, Tobias, but I cannot—I feel as though the sea is surging inside of me. The sea. . . ." Melvill tosses the crutch aside and runs toward the sea path, knowing it is a psychologically painful decision: He will view the ocean, its blue waves folding like bolts of silk, he will feel its wind on his face and arms—yet there will be no escape from the Typee Valley. Then he thinks, What if this is Providence? What if we discover a friendly ship moored in the harbor? Melvill pictures it there, a clipper with its sails secured at rest, only its flag—American or British or Australian—whipping in the breeze. It feels good to work his legs. His lungs are taking in the still air without laboring. He assumes the pace of a long-distance runner through the verdant jungle and has no concept of the miles as his mind remains focused on the hope of a ship, which becomes more and more real to him. The sea path opens out of the jungle, and Melvill glances behind to see that more than Toby and Korykory are following him: several natives, adolescent boys mainly, have joined the mad race to the sea. Melvill is breathing hard and sweating—it stings his eyes—

but he cannot stop. The sea path slopes down between grassy hillocks to the wide plain. He notices gulls crisscrossing ahead of him, their wings arced and holding the wind like sails.

At last Melvill comes to the gun shack and slows to a walk. He wonders if the ancient Typee is still within keeping his vigil. There is the sea, not as blue as he was thinking. Only slightly winded, he walks to the edge of the plain, before the steep decline to the ocean. Toby and the island boys and Korykory are following behind like a restless mob.

Melvill observes every detail of the final quarter mile: the narrow brown path cutting through waving grasses, knee-high when perfectly upright, the whitesand beach, deserted except for a large piece of driftwood and the lonely gulls that float above the blue water: angels in search of lost souls. There is a dull throb at Melvill's hip but he disregards it and runs down the final hill. The tips of the tall grasses nip at his legs. Then there is sand underfoot. Melvill has almost forgotten the difficulty of running on the beach. But it feels good to move like this. He is in the wet sand and falling to his knees but not from exhaustion. A quest completed. The cool ocean rushes in and soaks him to the waist. Again. . . . A salty drop hits him on the cheek and rolls into the corner of his lips.

Perhaps because of the wind in his ears or because of the vigorous splashing of the Typee boys but for a moment Melvill does not recognize the sound filling the air around him, then he understands it is his laughter: deep, robust—like a fullmoon lunatic's baying. Melvill falls forward then onto his back in the surf, laughing laughing.

It is some time before he calms down, the sun a blinding white spot when he glances toward it. A gull, two gulls glide through his field of vision. The exhilaration of being fit has left him, taking with it his energies. It seems like a long long way back to Marheyo's settlement. Where is Toby? Korykory? Melvill turns onto his elbows and finds them sitting together on the beach, beyond the ocean's reach, facing him. They are silently watching him—or past him, to the sea, to oblivion. Korykory's waistcloth has fallen aside and his prick is in plain view, lying on the white sand like a dead darkscaled fish.

As Melvill pushes himself upright he fully realizes his folly. The pain is spreading from his hip joint, and there is already a limp in his gait. Toby and Korykory are standing brushing themselves off. He thinks to say to Toby, "I was foolish," but there is no need. By the time Melvill reaches the gun shack he needs Toby's help to continue. Leaning heavily on his friend Melvill slowly presses on. The island boys at first were following but now, impatient, they rush ahead and are quickly out of sight past the hillocks.

Melvill is losing touch. At some point Korykory takes him and that is how he completes the journey—semiconscious on the Typee's strong back, like the first days in the valley. In Marheyo's hut Melvill swallows the coconut milk that is dribbled into his mouth then he gives in to the darkness overtaking his mind. It is complete. Like the deepest bowel of the *Acushnet*. Like the crypt.

eight

~~~~~~

Foolish, foolish: the self-reproach when he awakes and finds that his leg is reinjured. Consumed by the fever again, he has slept nearly twenty-four hours. Of course he would be ill again! Why could he not take it slowly and allow himself to regain his strength gradually? His impulsiveness again. Signing on with a whaler, then jumping ship and becoming trapped here with these cannibals. Melvill swears that if he can ever get home he will exorcise the rashness from his character—like a thirst for liquor or a passion for gambling.

After breakfast Toby heads for the Ti and Melvill awaits Fayaway's visit—perhaps the only bright streak to his relapse. Melvill is weak from the fever but a little food has revitalized him somewhat. Melvill lies in Marheyo's hut anticipating Fayaway, her smile, her warmth, her natural beauty. Soon she is there with the tortoise-shell of ointment. Melvill is ready for the treatment; his leg is fully bared.

As she starts at his toes Melvill says, "I should've let you work your magic yesterday and not run off halfcocked."

Fayaway says something in return—maybe she understands a little. She continues to chatter as she works the ointment into his ankle and calf muscle. Already the tingling is in his foot and toes, each small joint separately hot. The balm is doing its work and soothing the pain but its heat seems to be traveling to his brain making him even more feverish. As Fayaway's practiced hands encircle his patella his arousal intensifies. He does not attempt to distract his mind this time. Melvill allows himself an odd pleasure in the discomfort as he strains against the folded sheet. Up and down, as the instinct in his blood battles weight and gravity.

Fayaway talks on—much more than usual. Her strange island words make as much sense as his own thoughts: confused and digging back to a time before language.

She dips her hand into the ointment and begins with renewed vigor at his thigh. The space between her working fingers and his genitals is all the space in the world. His mind occupies that small space willing it to close. Suddenly her finger grazes his right testicle—a misstroke she has not made before. Her hands are high on his thigh . . . then again her small finger running along the curve of his testicle. He is nearly mad with want; yet paralyzed too. His heart and his cock pound with the same ferocity.

Fayaway stops and Melvill knows she is going to leave. He looks at her face and their eyes become fixed—like lovers', like fighters'. Saying nothing now she folds back the tappa sheet. With one hand, still sticky with the ointment, she cups Melvill's scrotum, gently squeezing; she places one finger of the other hand just below the head and begins to rub slowly. She had located a spot, a nerve that is beyond pleasure and is pure sexual intensity. In seconds the lower half of his body convulses, and a hot bead strikes Melvill on the cheek as the copious remainder bubbles onto his stomach. The smell of the salty Pacific fills his nostrils. He wants to reach out to Fayaway but he is inanimate and she is quickly gone.

It is some time before Melvill realizes there is commotion outside. At first he thinks it is in response to Fayaway and him. He uses the tappa sheet to clean himself then dresses. With the aid of the crutch he hobbles out. Natives are rushing here and there but no one pays attention to Melvill, which settles his fear and guilt regarding Fayaway. An old woman, moving at a slower pace, passes him; he says, "What's happening?" He gestures all around at the tumult. Maybe she understands, as she gives a precise but worthless response.

A young boy rushes past with a basket full of fruits. Melvill follows as quickly as he can. His leg is of no use, like lumber he is dragging. He is sweating and short of breath, yet there is still an odd bit of euphoria remaining from his encounter with Fayaway, the burden of desire temporarily lifted. He cannot fully grasp what is happening. A second boy, this one bearing a load of bamboo, passes him. Melvill watches the boy enter the ring of trees around the Ti and he disappears.

When Melvill finally reaches the grove only old men and women remain. He is hoping to find Toby but he is gone. Marheyo and Tinor are there. "Where is everyone?"

Marheyo says something and points to the sea path. Melvill is still confused, so Marheyo steps over to a nearby log and removes an ax with a metal head. He speaks more words and gestures again toward the sea path.

Melvill's mind tries to fit it all together: Is it possible a ship has come to their harbor and they are trading for goods?

Panicked, Melvill asks about Toby. Marheyo's vine-covered arm points to the sea path again. Melvill hurries as well as he can toward the sea. Surely Toby will secure passage for them both, if he can reach the ship at all. His friend would not abandon him here. The air of the jungle path feels cold; Melvill knows it is the sweat that drenches him. It worries him further that no more natives are running past him with their wares, as if the previous were the stragglers and the trading has been in progress for some time. . . .

And Toby? Damn it, where is Toby?

Melvill's crutch sticks in a depression and he tumbles onto the forest path. Still so far away from the pounding sea and he is exhausted. He is deaf except for the drumming of the salty blood in his ears. Toby. . . .

He thinks of the first time he understood that Toby and he were kindred spirits aboard the *Acushnet*. Taggart has all hands up top; he believes someone has stolen from the ship's stores. He does not say what, though, nor when. He simply struts to and fro with that ungodly leather in his hand. He has a flogging in mind, like a damned military ship. Melvill wonders if the mean bastard is inventing the entire story to scratch his sadistic itch for violence and blood. Melvill follows Taggart's back as he slowly passes the line of sailors. It is a beautiful sunny day on the ocean, in contrast to the grotesqueness of the whaler. Before Taggart turns, Melvill makes eye contact with Tobias Greene, who occupies the bunk above his. They exchange whole paragraphs in that momentary glance: the madness of what is happening, their mutual hatred for Taggart, the fucker's lust for violence, the fucker's lust. There is great comfort in that connection—someone shares Melvill's view, someone who is not a thief nor cutthroat nor rapist.

Toby.

Melvill gets to his feet and makes another agonizing mile, to where the jungle begins to open, when he encounters the first of the returning Typees, some carrying ax heads and longbladed knives. "Is the ship gone?" Melvill is desperate for an answer but the natives walk around him. He repeats himself again and again. A few natives smile at him obliviously. He must press on, he must see for himself. He manages another quarter mile or so before he meets Korykory on the path. "I must know: where is Toby?"

The words about Toby are indecipherable but the facial gestures, the diverting of his luminous brown eyes, are quite clear: Toby is gone.

Melvill knows he is about to collapse but there is nothing to be done about it—life and time and fate roll over him like a brutal wave bearing him down to a cold black sea.

nine

~~~~~

Hours pass. Days. Melvill has only a precarious foothold in reality, alive only in a small place within himself. The Typees do what they can for him, in *there*, but he responds with the barest animal instinct for survival. He swallows the sustenance they pour into his mouth; he uses the crude pots they bring him for his toilet. Once, twice Fayaway washes his inanimate body in Marheyo's hut. Melvill understands, without thinking it, it is for the native family's sake as much as for his.

At times Melvill is there in the hut alone with these cannibals. At times he is in the fetid *Acushnet* waiting for his shift to be rang on deck. In New York listening for the sound of his mother coming upstairs to rouse him for school. Always the funny nonsensical words drift down to him and settle strangely on his stomach. And on his heart.

A parade of visitors wanders past him—Melvill has the impression of an official corpse lying in state. The shuffling of bare feet over the mats and bamboo as the strangers move around him. The voices bearing the nonsensical words again. The voices are like music—plodding Protestant hymns—deep full tones with such a slow rhythm one thinks each note is the last. Until finally there is a last note lingering in the air. His mind tries to make the notes into a familiar pattern: "Are You Washed in the Blood?" "Rock of Ages," "Ye Ransomed Sinners, Hear." Vacuous time passes and Melvill begins to imagine the words of the hymns mingling with the labored Typee melody.

After a while he realizes the English is not his imagination at all—and the Typee words are not the slow notes of a song. Melvill opens his eyes and there is an oddly dressed native kneeling next to him. He is saying, "Hermes man to wake now . . . Hermes man to wake now. . . ."

Finally Melvill interrupts the long string of words. "I'm awake—you speak English." His voice is a whisper.

"Yes I know the English some." The native smiles broadly. He is not Typee; his skin is darker and the bone structure of his face more angular; and he does not have the Typees' small flat nose. He wears the Typee warrior's sharktooth necklace but he also has on a kind of buttonless red vest and bands of woven grass around each biceps.

"Who are you?" Melvill manages. His throat is dry.

"My name is called Marnoo." Again the flash of the broad smile. "I come to speak for you."

". . . for me . . ." Melvill is voiceless.

Marnoo signals to someone standing in the shadows beyond Melvill's vision. Melvill expects Korykory or Marheyo to come forth but it is a young boy who brings a cup of water. As the boy helps Melvill drink he notices the three dots on the boy's forehead. He has seen the tattooing before: on the dried heads of the Happar warriors in the Ti. The cool water is delicious and revitalizes Melvill some. He sits up with Marnoo's assistance.

"How long have I been asleep?"

Marnoo understands the real point of Melvill's question and says, "Your friend is gone to near five days." He holds up his hand, the fingers and thumb spread.

Melvill puts his head down—it is true then and not just a terrible dream.

Marnoo anticipates his next question: "Sailing men like you come to trade, your mate speaks then goes with them to the ship." Again Marnoo anticipates: "They sail away—the Typee say the white sails sink into the ocean."

Melvill sits quietly for a moment before Marnoo says,

"Come. Daylight give you the strength." He helps Melvill stand and hands him his crutch. It is mid to late afternoon. The village is peaceful. Melvill hears the voices of children at play. His leg is stiff but there is little pain. He and Marnoo sit on a log next to the firepit. The sun, slightly filtered by the jungle, does begin to enliven him.

Marnoo rearranges the longbladed knife that hangs at his side as he crosses his legs. "The old ones they send for me when your mate he goes."

"Who are you? You're not Typee. And how is it you speak English?"

"I am Marnoo. Marnoo is talker, hearer—" he touches his lips, his ears—"for all men on island. Typee they cannot talk to Happar, Happar they cannot talk to Typee. Happar Typee they cannot talk to Uahanna, Uahanna they cannot talk to Nukuheva and so and so. When a boy I picked to be Marnoo. Like this boy. Boy Marnoo too."

"So you are an interpreter for the entire island, a diplomatic envoy for life. And you learned English as well?"

"When Marnoo become a man Marnoo not want to be Marnoo. Become harpooner on Aussie whaleship the *Sarah Jones*. Harpoon whales six months. But Marnoo get chance to be Marnoo again. I come back."

"Lucky for me I guess. I don't understand the Typees—why are they so protective of me?"

"You and mate come from mountains where the sun lives. All other sailing men come from the sea. You special. Harming you taboo. Some say you bring luck to Typees. They say you go and it taboo."

"And Toby leaving, is that taboo?"

"Your mate go you here—no Typee can say. Some say you go some say stay. Many . . . hot words about you go you stay."

"Will Marnoo help me to go?"

"Marnoo not here to help or hurt. Marnoo here to talk and hear. Hermes man like Toby man make his own path. Gods say if good or bad."

"It's 'Herman' by the by. The Typees can't seem to say that."

"Great Happar chief Manoa he kill many many Typee before Typee kill Manoa. 'Herman' sound like 'Manoa' to Typee: taboo."

"Well, 'Hermes' can't go anywhere now." Melvill pats his bad leg.

"Yes. Some Typee say gods put sickness in your leg so you staying. Some say gods punish you for you not going."

"Then why does Fayaway nurse me if it's the gods' sickness?"

"Father of Fayaway great warrior. Gods' magic with him all time. Fayaway maybe she help gods' sickness and no get gods' sickness." Marnoo suddenly stands up. "Must go now."

"Wait—what am I to do? I don't want to stay here forever."

"Marnoo not here to help or hurt. . . ."

"I know, only to talk and hear—well go ahead and talk. I'm listening." He rakes back his hair and touches his ear.

The islander thinks for a moment, a half smile on his thin lips. "Trust in Fayaway. She close to gods. By Fayaway you know what to do."

Melvill was hoping for advice a bit less like a riddle. He stands with the aid of the crutch. "Thank you, Marnoo. Please don't be far away." He offers his hand.

Marnoo hesitates a moment, not accustomed to handshakes on the island, then accepts Melvill's with a brief firm grip. Marnoo departs with his young novice. A dozen Typee children come from nowhere to hop along at their heels. The Pied Piper, thinks Melvill. When Marnoo is out of sight and the sound of the children has died down, the bewilderment returns to Melvill. One action at a time, day by day, hour by hour: this is how you must deal with it, he instructs himself.

Even modest exercise makes him feel less weak. He decides to go downstream to the bathing pool. There are several Typees there—some adults, some children. Melvill strips off his clothes and wades into the cool water. He gently paddles to the far side then pulls himself onto the sandy bank. The sun glows red inside the lids of his closed eyes and its heat penetrates him completely. His hunger growls and he runs his fingers along the protrusions of ribs. Except for the meal of roasted boar, his diet has been vegetarian. Melvill has never been so thin, not even as a sometimes sickly boy.

He recalls the poverty of his adolescence. It was never the poverty of hunger but rather the poverty of shame. The aura of dread and failure following the family to Albany—the widow and her eight children—the great city claiming them victim, his dead father's business collapsed in spite of his eldest brother's tireless efforts. The terrible economy affecting everything, lurking everywhere. And his searching for a career—keeping shop, teaching, surveying, farming—which would lead him west to Illinois then finally to New Bedford and whaling as a last resort: a family tradition to go to sea.

And now he has failed at that too.

Melvill rolls over to peer into a shallow puddle among some rocks at the edge of the stream. He is surprised by the wild face that reflects back at him: the long unruly hair, the black untrimmed beard, and his face so gaunt that his eyes blaze back, overlarge. He turns his head to the side to verify that this is himself he sees—and not some image from a fever-induced hallucination. He thinks it is a wonder that Fayaway comes near him without armed escort.

He rolls onto his back again, places his arm over his face and allows the sound of the cataract to mesmerize him into sleep. He dreams of Mocha Dick, the whale who hunts whalemen, and about a man obsessed with revenge. Melvill is there on the deck of the ship, a sailor following the obsessed man in a black woolen cloak, trying desperately to see his face—but the man moves each time Melvill moves. This odd dance goes on and on, until Melvill realizes in his dream that he is not a sailor on the man's ship but rather he is the man's shadow: locked there by the highbright sun or nickelplated moon or brilliant oceansky stars … and by the physical laws of the natural world.…

He wakes with a start as a shadow falls across him—Korykory blocking the light and dripping icy drops from his swim.

t e n

~~~~~~

Food revives Melvill; it is a midday meal. He has found that his long convalescence has much improved his leg. He cautions himself to go slowly in order to make a full recovery and not to run to the sea like a lunatic. He thinks of Marnoo's advice: trust in Fayaway. Advice which is easy to follow.

When the meal is finished he goes out into the bright day. He brings his crutch but uses it more as a walkingstick. He wants to see Fayaway; however all this time on the island and he is not certain where she lives, only the general direction from which she comes. Perhaps it is the cluster of huts where Melvill was taken to see the slain warrior. It is not terribly far and if he proceeds slowly his leg should hold up, he hopes.

The day is excessively hot, even for the tropics. Melvill's shirt is unbuttoned and flaps completely open, the loose tail hanging down to nearly his knee. Something about the way the shirt is fitting reminds him of an oversized cloak his father used to wear in winter. He sees his father coming in from a day of business, removing the black cloak in the foyer, frost clinging to his mustache but already beginning to melt. His father smiling kindly beneath the large wet mustache. Then he sees his father's face inanimate and pale in death—that terrible black casket, dominating the parlor, that black casket that surfaces in Melvill's mind from time to time, always unexpectedly.

This path does not seem even remotely familiar to him. The path itself is unusual, with stones protruding from the earth like broken fingers. The stones are worn smooth and quite different underfoot from the volcanic sand that permeates most of the valley. Small birds—orange, bright blue, and yellow—flit back and forth in front of Melvill. Their small wings make no sound in the heavy moist air. The trees however seem less tropical, like those found in a more temperate climate. Melvill misses the fir trees of his home, and the hardwood oaks whose leaves paint the autumn landscape so majestically. This island is a beautiful place, he thinks, an Eden populated with a noble people—why then do I want so desperately to leave? Essentially, he thinks, this island in the South Pacific Ocean is not home; my family does not reside here, nor do they stem from here. It is that simple: home attracts him because it is home. Only his New York and his New England will settle him, will quell his restlessness. He had to sail across the globe and risk his life among these cannibals to finally understand.

Through the trees Melvill can see the first huts of this neighborhood cluster. Then in full view with the blue lake behind he sees mainly old women in the yard doing various chores, and the naked children playing. There are perhaps thirty huts which stretch two thirds around the oval lake. Melvill notices the stone slab where Toonoo's body lay in its final rest, he sees again the garland of white flowers. It is the children who notice and greet Melvill, running to him in a gleeful disorganized flock. He can hear his name—"Hermes . . . Hermes"—within their chatter. He is surprised at his celebrity. The children bounce around him as he continues to make his slow path. He cannot help noticing the girls who have begun to sprout buds of breasts. He decides to make use of the happy children: "Fayaway? Where can I find Fayaway?"

Instantly her name, perhaps with an air of celebrity too, cascades from the children. They herd him in a new direction. Women look up from their work for a moment as Melvill and the children pass, then they return unimpressed to their tasks. Steered by the boys and girls Melvill does not use his crutch at all.

They stop in front of a hut that is slightly larger than the ones nearest it. A girl, perhaps the oldest child there, approaches the hut's opening and speaks with someone inside. Melvill distinctly hears the girl giggle. In a moment Fayaway steps from the opening out into the daylight. Always her raw beauty astonishes him. She does not appear surprised to see him. She says something about his "*league*."

"Yes, doing better again." He gives his leg a hardy slap to emphasize its regained vitality. "I'm here to . . . Marnoo instructed me. . . ." He does not know what to say, even though he understands his precise words matter little.

But she does not make him stand there stammering any longer. Fayaway says something to the children and they run off chirping happily in their strange tongues. Like a big sister promising candy to her pestering younger siblings, thinks Melvill. Then Fayaway steps forward and gestures toward the lake.

"A capital idea—let's stroll near the lake." Its darkblue waters give it the appearance of depth, almost an oceanlike depth. They walk in silence for a while. Melvill notices the sunlight etching white ripples in the water. First he wishes Fayaway were an Englishspeaking girl; then he recalls his awkwardness with those girls too and is glad in a way that she comprehends only a little English. He thinks about his foolish shyness with the New Bedford whore Madeline who kindly inquired about his specific wants until she understood his greenness and directed the whole affair herself. He thinks about the softness of Madeline's breasts, a tiny brown mole on the left one, the one that she held to his lips to begin, and how they smelled of beer as her last customer, only minutes departed, must have had it thick on his breath.

Arousal begins in Melvill and he forces himself to think of more mundane subjects, the shape of the clouds overhead, what types of fish might dwell in the lake—and to not look at Fayaway, even peripherally, because it only increases his physical discomfort.

In some tall grass by the lake's edge is a small canoe with one crude paddle resting on its upturned bottom. "A boat," says Melvill, thankful for the diversion. "We must take it out on the lake." He steps over to the canoe.

Fayway begins protesting, her alien words obviously in the negative.

"It's all right. I think I can handle a miniature canoe." He exchanges his crutch for the paddle. He has some difficulty flipping over the canoe: it has been resting there a long time and has made a deep impression in the sandy bank. Underneath the grass is dead and some viny weeds are growing in a tangle.

Meantime Fayaway's protestations have been increasing, and Melvill can now decipher the word "taboo."

"Ah, you people and your taboos," he says, beginning to feel annoyed, then he recalls Marnoo's explanation that it was the Typees' superstitiousness that prevented them from hacking Toby and him to death when they arrived. "It's all right," says Melvill, patient again but stubborn. "Nothing is going to happen." It must not be too taboo, he thinks, if the canoe is here in the first place.

Fayaway is obviously perplexed. Her pretty face is contorted with anxiety.

Melvill puts the canoe in the lake and steps in as it glides into deeper water. He uses the paddle to slow its departure. "You see—it's fine." He motions to Fayaway to join him but she is resolute on the bank, as fixed as those viny weeds in the soil. He paddles a bit farther and repeats his assurances.

She holds her pose for a moment then suddenly marches forward into the water. Melvill thinks she has changed her mind but she quickly unties the short white cloth at her waist, tosses it to the bank, and dives into the lake. She swims as effortlessly as a dolphin underwater, her narrow brown buttocks just brushing the surface. Fayaway slips past Melvill in the canoe and rises to take a breath; then she is stroking toward the deep center of the lake leaving Melvill behind. He sees the white soles of her kicking feet as he turns the canoe and paddles hard to try to catch her. When Fayaway reaches the middle she rolls over to float on her back.

Melvill stops paddling as he nears her. "You're an amazing swimmer."

She is squinting against the sun but smiles up at him as if she understands the compliment. Her long black hair is fanned out on the water, like a creature in its natural habitat. As Fayaway closes her eyes against the sun Melvill gazes at the small black patch between her gently kicking legs: it is essentially the only part of her anatomy he has not seen, which amplifies its natural hold on his imagination. Melvill looks back at Fayaway's face to find her staring at him. He cannot read her expression. She instantly turns onto her stomach and dives under the canoe. She goes so deep Melvill can barely see her sleek form. Then she disappears altogether and he begins notching the seconds in his mind. Fifteen seconds . . . a half a minute. . . . Fayaway is under water so long he starts to be concerned. Should he go in after her? Should he call for help? Suddenly she pops up an astonishing distance from the canoe. She smiles and waves at Melvill before diving under again. He notes the sighting, the last glimpse of her, Fayaway's feet, her toes pointing toward the sun, and begins paddling in her direction. But he is only halfway when Fayaway surfaces again, at a right angle to Melvill's canoe. Again she smiles and waves before plunging down.

Melvill says, "This is obviously a game you wish to play," but there is no point to his remark.

Melvill maneuvers toward her newest set of concentric circles to demonstrate some interest in the game. This time she shows herself to his left, not quite as distant as she has been— perhaps she is finally tiring. She waves, less vigorously, before going underwater. Melvill turns the canoe toward her last appearance but does not bother working the paddle, only using it as a rudder to stay straight.

A longer period of time elapses and Melvill starts to worry again. He thinks of young Jones from the *Acushnet* and of the search boats that circled aft even into the night, their lanterns like the yellow eyes of seamonsters in the gloom.

Fayaway comes up panting at the side of the canoe. In her right hand she is holding something while she grips the canoe with her left. It takes Melvill a moment to realize it is a black snake partially curled around her wrist.

Melvill tries to disguise his aversion while Fayaway chatters excitedly, having quickly regained her breath. She seems to be telling about the snake or how she came to catch it. It is thicker than Fayaway's thumb. He hopes she does not intend to hand him the snake or even put it in the boat. He envisions girlishly beating the snake to death with the paddle.

With a final flourish of commentary, Fayaway releases the snake into the water. It skims along the surface with impressive speed, leaving no trail.

Melvill looks back to Fayaway and again she is staring at him, not smiling but not severe either—another of those Typee masks he cannot fathom.

There are voices calling from the shore. A small group of islanders is beckoning them, or just Fayaway. "Looks like—" Melvill begins but Fayaway is already stroking toward her clansmen. Her buttocks and legs working smoothly—tirelessly it would seem.

Fayaway reaches shore before him and he suspects that the group will instantly absorb her and he will be left alone. But after the briefest conversation Fayaway is there by herself on the bank waiting for him, tying on her white skirt. He notices that all the ablebodied men are leaving the cluster of huts together. Is another battle to ensue? However there is no urgency in their departure. They might have been a group of churchgoers strolling to Sunday worship. He tries to imagine the Typees in dark woolen clothing, Bibles in hand. The picture will not take

The Canoe

shape. They appear to be headed toward the hub of the Typee Valley, toward Marheyo's cluster of huts or the Ti grove itself.

Melvill pulls the canoe on to the bank and replaces it as nearly as possible to its previous resting place then he retrieves his crutch from the tall grass and uses it for its intended purpose. He can feel the effects of the exertion on his hip joint, where the malady seems to have localized.

"I should most likely go home, back to Marheyo's."

Fayaway shakes her head no, smiles and urges him in another direction.

"My leg is starting to feel inflamed again." He pats his hip.

She says something, mentioning his "*league*," but urges him again.

Marnoo's advice—trust in Fayaway—returns to him. Behind the hut where he found her is an obscure path, narrow and shaded. The path itself seems to be of smooth stone, uphill, and it is not quite wide enough for them to walk abreast; Fayaway is slightly ahead and moves at an angle. There is an otherworldliness to the path. The air feels cooler, less tropical, and the bird and insect sounds are not the same. They are more like echoes—the echoes of extinct species, he thinks. Melvill favors his good leg as they tread onward. He wishes that he had stayed in Marheyo's hut allowing his leg to recover even further.

The vegetation on the lefthand side of the path ends abruptly revealing a wall of rock that extends straight up and disappears in the thick leafy canopy. Soon the path ends altogether, slightly wider at its terminus. Fayaway, who has been perfectly quiet, begins talking and gesturing toward the wall of stone. Melvill listens intently to her words but they are as enigmatic as always. Then he realizes there is a shape in the stone that the gloom has helped to conceal. At first it looks naturally formed. But no, some hand has been at work chipping and smoothing. It is a large face, broad and thick-lipped like the Typees, and nearly as tall as Melvill, its forehead almost even with Melvill's, its chin at his feet. Its eyes are two palm-size circles. The left eye is less distinct, partially eroded, giving the impression there is a membrane over the pupil, making the carving half blind.

"Boolaa," Fayaway is saying. "Boolaa."

Melvill repeats the strange word. It must be one of their many gods.

Fayaway runs her fingers near the carving, especially its large eyes but she never touches it, Melvill notes. Taboo no doubt. Fayaway begins to back away from Boolaa and Melvill reacts to follow. She stops him and gestures more dramatically toward the wall. Fayaway wants him to stay there—with this bizarre god who stares expressionless into an impenetrable jungle—while she returns down the path.

"I would prefer not to."

Fayaway pays no attention as she turns her back to him and vanishes into the dusky path.

Melvill peers into Boolaa's eyes, circles in a pair of rough-hewn squares. He risks the taboo and touches the partly eroded eye. He expects the stone to feel cool but it is warm, which startles him. Some sort of subterranean heat that gives the impression the stone god is alive.

Boolaa, who are you to these people? Their god of the mountain, the jungle? Of narrow footpaths? Of lonesome stonecarvers? I don't know what Fayaway expects me to do here. If you were the face of my God, what would I say? Ask? But who's to say you aren't my God, secluded here on this remote island, in this valley of cannibals, and not in the confines of some New England worshiphouse, nor in Rome?

Melvill smiles at the sacrilege, the heresy.

He steps back to gain a fuller view of the face. It looks slightly malevolent close but loses some of its harshness with distance. He studies the deeply grooved lines. Their darkness seems to move, to flow in and around the face, like black blood through a primitive circulatory system.

Well, Boolaa, in lieu of my God . . . what do I do to get home? What path do I follow? Melvill realizes the broader question:

If I get home, what then? What new line for my failure? What new enterprise with which to sink?

Pain suddenly surges through his leg, like a wave at high tide, and he drops to his knees and hands, the crutch pinned to the hard ground. Melvill looks into the closed lips of Boolaa. The idol's silence surrounds him, thunderously. Yes, first things first. First to get off this island. Out of this valley of cannibals. He stares into Boolaa's stone face. No answers. No compass. No sextant. No astrolabe. He looks up along the wall of rock and verdant canopy: no sky, no sun, no stars. . . .

Something cold pricks him on the cheek. Again, again. Drops of water. It is raining up there somewhere on the mountain, and water is running and falling along its cracks and crevices to find him there kneeling before Boolaa. Water is streaking Boolaa's face, especially the eroded eye. The god appears to be crying. Melvill touches his own face, where rainwater has dampened his beard. Here I am: weeping with this ancient god.

When Melvill returns down the path he finds Fayaway waiting. They return to Fayaway's hut and Melvill departs alone, leaning heavily on his crutch.

The path is quite desolate—even the fauna are subdued. Melvill aches to hear Toby call out to him *old fellow*, proving this isolation some terrible dream. But where would he wake? With Toby but still among the cannibals? With Toby but still aboard the wretched whaleship? Or another ship but still thousands of miles from home? Back in Albany with the family's sickly business and his mother who seems determined to mourn forever?

There are so many layers to his nightmare, like a rotten onion, it seems futile to wish for deliverance. However, natural instinct for survival is still at his core driving him . . . to seek a way from this valley . . . this island . . . this ocean.

Finally he reaches Marheyo's cluster of huts. Only Tinor and the other old women are there; even the children are away.

The God Weeps

Tinor, who is crouched next to a friend removing berries from some jungle sprig, acknowledges Melvill with a glance and a nod. No words.

"Where are the men? Where are the children?" Melvill holds his free hand at waist level to try to communicate children.

Of course there is no response. His leg is sore though not as bad as he feared it might become. His curiosity, combined with anxiety, pushes him on. He suspects the Ti grove is a likely place to look for a mass gathering. He digs his crutch into the ground and moves ahead. He does not go far when he determines his suspicions were on target. Ahead in the grove he can see movement through the trees, and he can hear an occasional childish shout, which spurs him on.

Passing among the trees the air is cooler and he is tempted to stop and rest but keeps going. The clearing in the center of the buildings is teeming with children at play. Melvill has barely emerged from the trees when one child sees him, calls out, and suddenly they are all around him, gaily corralling him toward the middle of the grove. He tries to quiet them. He wants to know where their fathers and grandfathers are. He wants to know what is happening.

He halts near the center. The children are swarming everywhere around him—dozens of them—some holding hands circling him, some simply running to and fro, shouting, calling out, "Her-meez!"

Melvill continues to try to calm them. He looks up at the Ti. This is where the men have assembled. They are apparently packed tightly into the overlarge hut, standing room only. The youngest men, boys really, have spilled out onto the portico. Their attention is suddenly divided between what is happening inside and the children's playful riot. Melvill wonders if he is the cause of it all. Are the men discussing him inside the Ti? What are they concluding? Melvill's throat tightens, as if caught in a snare. Perhaps he is merely overthirsty.

He makes his way to a log to rest. The children soon lose

interest in him and scamper into other games. Words thick with emotion belch from inside the Ti. Their denotations are lost on him but their connotations seem clear: sometimes sympathetic, sometimes hostile, and other times merely inquisitive. Occasionally one of the boys on the portico glances over at him. Melvill wishes he had a book or a newspaper, anything to focus his attention—rather than just sit there staring like a cat in the yard, swishing his tail at an interesting moth.

At length the meeting adjourns and men file out of the Ti and down its stone base. They come and come, more men inside than Melvill could have imagined. Many seem to notice him, many do not. At last a familiar face, Korykory walks up to him and says some phrase in greeting. The young islander then tries to explain something, something in the sky, but not the sun, Melvill gathers. Is Korykory just making conversation or is this information truly important to Melvill. He cannot say. Marheyo joins them. The old man is somber as always. Mehevi, the chief, passes and smiles broadly at Melvill. Melvill takes it as a good sign and begins to feel more at ease—until Mowmow, the one-eyed warrior captain, also passes and glares at Melvill with his solitary orb, his provoking bull's-eye. Melvill thinks of the Greek hero Ulysses and his battle with the Cyclops, and Melvill wishes for the Greek's strength and cunning.

Korykory encourages Melvill to rise, and they turn toward Marheyo's hut. Melvill limps on his now stiff leg. Korykory, seeing this, instantly takes Melvill onto his back. So again Melvill watches the birds on Korykory's muscular shoulders take flight.

eleven

~~~~~

After lunch Melvill rests. He tries to sleep but cannot quite achieve it. The Typees' division over him, the hostile stare of Mowmow's single eye, Melvill's desire to be with Fayaway—it all adds to his restlessness. He imagines where Toby might be. On a cutter slicing through the cerulean ocean bound for home. Melvill cannot at first stem the envy and the anger. It is possible that Toby's ship is anchored at Nukuheva and that his friend is concocting a plan at this moment to rescue him. Melvill cannot force himself to believe it.

This cycle of thinking persists for some time. It is late afternoon when Korykory fetches him. He gestures to Melvill to leave the hut with him. Melvill is relieved to discover his leg feels good with only the faintest twinge of discomfort. He takes his crutch though.

"Where are we going?"

Korykory sensing Melvill's meaning waves vaguely toward the Ti.

It's too early for supper, Melvill thinks. Maybe the verdict has been reached and I'm being led to the gallows. No, Melvill cannot believe the kindhearted Korykory would accept such a task. The village is unusually quiet. Normally women would be starting the preparation of meals and the ubiquitous children would be playing. There are a few natives about but they are generally idle—much like the old men who hold daily vigil in front of the tobacconist's shop in Albany. They seem to be either in heated debate amid their haze of smoke or in deep introspective reverie.

Melvill follows Korykory to the Ti grove then onto the path which led to the cannibal's feast, the recollection of which makes Melvill uneasy. Soon however they divert to a different path, narrower and with even denser vegetation, one that Melvill has not noted before. The jungle here is filled with colorful flowers: luminous yellow, red, orange, violetblue—starkly contrasting against the dark dark green. Their scents are equally potent. Some overpoweringly sweet, some fetid.

The jungle recedes a bit and there is a hut. As soon as it is revealed Korykory calls out and a native steps from its opening. The man's tattooed face and body surprise and repulse Melvill. It is difficult to locate a patch of skin that is not dyed with some elaborate design. When he smiles in greeting the whites of his teeth and his eyes are vivid against his densely illustrated skin.

Korykory and the man speak excitedly together, old friends perhaps. The man's age is difficult to reckon because of the elaborate tattooing but certainly he is older than Korykory. Suddenly they are talking about Melvill. Korykory puts his hand on Melvill's shoulder, *Hermes this* and *Hermes that.*

The tattooed islander calls into his hut and immediately a boy emerges with two large baskets. The boy, twelve or thirteen, appears free of tattoos. He carries the baskets to a crude bench as Melvill is urged toward the bench too. Korykory tugs at Melvill's shirt for him to remove it. Standing beside the bench now Melvill can see that the baskets contain bowls of dark fluids, cloth, and wooden needles.

"Oh no. Thank you but no thank you. I prefer no tattoos at this time." He shakes his head vigorously declining the offer.

He tries to back away but Korykory has a firm grip on his shirt. The young Typee becomes very animated as he implores Melvill to sit. His mood is serious—not that of a schoolmate urging a dare. It is as if everything depends on Melvill's cooperation. Korykory, still chattering excitedly, covers one eye and glares at Melvill.

"This has something to do with Mowmow?" Melvill covers one eye.

Korykory affirms Melvill's inference then is silent.

Melvill looks down at the basket of needles. "If this has something to do with Mowmow then my future may depend on it." He removes his shirt.

The tattooist, named Karky apparently, examines Melvill enthusiastically running his bony fingers over Melvill's white shoulders, chest, shoulder blades: a virgin canvas for his needle and ink. Karky seems to have no interest in Melvill's tanned forearms and hands. He and Korykory enter into a lively discussion; Karky keeps looking to Melvill as if he might join in.

"I still would prefer not—truly."

The Typees reach consensus on some issue. Karky prods and pinches Melvill's right shoulder, just beyond his sight. If they must, it is an all right location, thinks Melvill glancing at the bunch of wooden needles. Karky sits Melvill down on the rough bench and calls to his assistant, who comes with a cup for Melvill. By its smell he knows it is their "arva-wai"—no doubt to help him bear the stick of the needle. He takes a sip of the awful brew. Wormwood, he thinks.

Almost instantly the potent drink goes to his head. Meanwhile Karky is washing his skin in various fluids preparing it. The fluids feel cool and make his skin tingle. A few more sips of the arva-wai and Melvill loses nearly all sensation. He can feel some pressure and pulling at his shoulder but no real pain. And he does not care what Karky is doing back there. With all the poking and pulling he imagines a vibrant Mexican mural on his back and it is all right.

"Be sssure t'render a radianGuadelupe," Melvill slurs.

Korykory takes hold of his arm and Melvill understands it is to stop his swaying even though he cannot sense his own movement. He takes a big drink of the arva-wai. Korykory takes the sloshing cup from his hands.

Melvill sits there for some time totally immersed in the activity of riding the bench. He has difficulty recalling why he is there. Occasionally he thinks it is Fayaway holding his arm and is disappointed each time to locate Korykory there smiling at him. Though he cannot feel its prick, he knows when the needle is piercing his skin and he remembers the harpoons in the thick hides of the whales, how much force it took to bury the weapon's sharp head into a vital organ, the death sound of the animals when they sensed their mortality, their blowholes ejaculating pure blood. . . . Then somehow he knows it is the image of a whale that has been inked into his skin, a blue outline on his white canvas. He senses the needle as Karky renders a representation of that enigmatic eye, that probing judgmental eye.

That eye.

(•)

Melvill is holding onto the image, that eye, when he slips from consciousness altogether.

twelve

~~~

The dream is always the same.

Sometime in the ninth month at sea the dream came to him. The idea—the hope—of Taggart's being dead had been with him for a while, like a mole you have forgotten until you discover it again. To see a tackle and imagine it swinging loose into the unsuspecting head of Taggart, to think of a wave surging over the bow where Taggart is standing imperiously, to envision a whale crushing Taggart's boat during a hunt: these are normal thoughts. Toby has them too, no doubt others as well. But in the dream Melvill is the instrument of Taggart's destruction. First a harpoon through the abdomen to pin Taggart to the main mast. He writhes like an insect to be free. It is futile however and Melvill has no thought of mercy. Then Melvill has the knife, the big whale-knife, the one used for carving up the giant fish. Melvill begins by cutting the clothes from Taggart's thrashing body. His gaudy silver beltbuckle hits the deck like the report of a pistol. Melvill looks for fear in the bastard's eyes but sees none and is disappointed. Then he starts to peel the pink flesh from Taggart's bones. It comes off like old wallpaper. The foul stench of whale blubber fills the air. Is the air. A wave comes over the gunwale and washes the deck clean of Taggart's skin and clothes, even the heavy ornate buckle. The blade comes to Taggart's pecker, which squirms like an independent beast. Finally there is fear in the chiefmate's eyes. Satisfied now, Melvill puts the bloody knife point to Taggart's throat. . . .

The dream is always the same. It is his own murderous thoughts that frighten Melvill. The violence that lurks inside him.

thirteen

~~~

When Melvill awakes, Marheyo and Tinor are quite busy, but illuminated by only the bluish light from a pair of tapers it is difficult to tell what they are busy about. Besides, Melvill's head is throbbing and he has a terrible thirst—reminiscent of when he and Toby descended from the wild mountains into this valley. How many days before? Impossible to say. Melvill closes his eyes and even this is painful.

Marheyo must have seen him stir. The old man speaks to Melvill and brings him a large cup of water. Melvill sits up to drink, which increases the pounding in his brain. Melvill reaches for the cup and feels the dull pain pulling at his shoulder: the tattoo. He had nearly forgotten. He wants to see it but that would require removing his shirt and more light, possibly even a mirror, not one of which he has seen since leaving the *Acushnet*. He takes a long drink of the tepid water and it is delicious.

Marheyo cautions him to slow down or to wait a moment then he goes to the far side of the hut where the family's stores are kept. He returns with a bowl, takes Melvill's cup, drops a pinch of white powder from the bowl into the water, swirls it, and returns the cup to Melvill—says something about "arva" and points to Melvill's head.

Melvill drinks. It is bitter and grainy and smells a bit like greenwillow bark. Marheyo encourages him to drink it all, which he does with effort.

Then Korykory is at the doorway speaking to his parents. The old man and his son help Melvill to stand. It is nearly dusk outside. They begin to make their way toward the Ti grove. The whole family and other families too, but not all. Melvill's leg is not bad and they make good progress. He uses the crutch more like a walkingstick.

In the grove other families merge with their large group. Fayaway is among the new arrivals. Like most of the females she is wearing a cape of white tappa. She naturally joins in with Melvill and Korykory. The mass of islanders forms narrower columns as they take the sea path. It is dim. Here and there natives raise lighted torches of coconut husks.

Melvill wants to know what is happening but he is not concerned for his safety. This is not a war party, nor an angry mob bent on his demise. In spite of the jungle's density the air becomes cooler and fresher as they advance toward the sea. Perhaps a ship is there waiting to take me from this island, Melvill allows himself to think for a moment, then dismisses it as utter fantasy.

The throng is strangely quiet as they make their way along the barely illuminated path. The torchbearers often reach down to replenish their flames with fuel that has fallen to the ground naturally. The group's pace is leisurely enough that even the elderly and the infirm have no trouble keeping up.

Melvill is delighted when he feels Fayaway's small hand lightly grip his arm. He imagines going to a New York City cotillion, and escorting his dark naked maiden onto the dancefloor. He smiles to think of the shockwave among the dowagers. Melvill looks down and discovers that Fayaway is holding Korykory's arm as well which beclouds his delight somewhat.

Night seems to lengthen the sea path but eventually they emerge from the dense jungle onto the high plain. All at once stars appear overhead and the thunderous sound of the surf reaches them. Ahead Melvill notices groups of Typee men shouldering long boats. Melvill does not know when the boats were retrieved, or if these are new groups of Typees who have rendezvoused here. A brilliant fullmoon gleams off the boat bottoms, seven in all. The entire beach and ocean surface are well lighted by the luminous white disk. The gun shack stands alone in the moonlight like a wearied sentry.

Once on the beach the columns of natives fan out. Melvill tries to stay with Korykory and Fayaway but Korykory breaks from them and runs toward one of the groups with a boat. While the natives with the boats advance toward the breaking waves, others use the torches to light fires on the beach, the wood piles having been prepared in advance.

Fayaway leads Melvill to one of the small fires. Someone has unfolded a large piece of tappa on the sand so Fayaway and Melvill sit. Melvill watches as the boats are launched into the ocean, each carrying a dozen Typee men outfitted with paddles, nets and spears. The long narrow boats seesaw on the waves for a moment then they are expertly guided into deep water.

Melvill did not know the Typees were mariners. He thinks about the sea spray flying, recalls the icy pinpricks on his skin.

The night is so clear and the moon so bright the boats can be seen a good distance on the open water. Melvill wants to stand to see even farther but this may be considered impolite. The men who had helped launch the boats have now taken seats around the various fires. The Typees are engaged in lively conversations. Every so often he can recognize a Typee word or phrase but for the most part they could be parrots chattering nonsense in the jungle or wildboars grunting in the undergrowth.

Melvill stares beyond the fishing boats to the limitless open sea. He thinks of Ulysses on the beach longing for home in spite of the company of a goddess, who is both captor and lover. He thinks of the leviathans who roam the cold oceans and of the infamous brute who hunts men, truly like the seamonsters of myth. It takes him a moment to recall the brute's name—Mocha Dick—and it bothers him: evidence that his former existence is fading from memory. And if its fading is complete did it ever truly exist?

The moon, large in the lavender sky, is near its zenith when the boats return one by one, each with its catch of fishes, silvery in the moonlight, like pieces-of-eight brought up from a sunken Spanish galleon. The nets are emptied onto sheets and Melvill expects the preparation of the fish to begin. He walks with Fayaway toward the wriggling bounty. He is shocked however when the Typees start eating the fish raw, skin, scales and all. Fayaway reaches down and selects a small silverorange fish and starts eating it hungrily. Scales glitter iridescently on her lips.

She finishes the flesh of her fish and tosses the remains on the sand. She smiles, her mouth shiny with gore, and hands Melvill a fish, slightly larger than the one she just consumed.

It is still cold from the sea, some variety of perch, he thinks. Moonlight catches its eye and enlivens it for a brief moment, amplifying his repulsion. But the sounds of dozens of Typees enjoying the catch, rarely talking in fact they are so enthralled by this midnight-hour meal, settles Melvill. He brings the fish to his lips and nibbles at the fleshy part near its lateral fin, only enough to break the skin, and he tastes the saltiness. He rents the skin by pulling at the fin, exposing the meat, radiant beneath the fullmoon. Melvill bites at it and is surprised by the richness of the flavor. He eats more, enjoying it, glad to have animal flesh after so many meals of fruit, mashed or chopped or straight from the tree. It reminds him of the beefsteak Toby and he discussed having when reaching the Hawaiian Islands, now so long ago, like a conversation from a dream only vaguely recollected.

Melvill looks around him, and at his pretty Fayaway: a primitive people performing a primitive ritual, as unchanged as copulating and excreting and birthing, all the natural acts of a living species. If I stay long enough, will I partake of human flesh? He assures himself no but there is a residue of doubt in his mind. Only moments ago he was repulsed by the idea of

Glittering Scales

eating the raw fish, and now. . . .

He tosses the carcass of his fish on the beach—it will be a good meal for a scavenger bird, plenty of flesh still clinging to the skeleton, and the entrails too. He imagines the bird that will be reflected in the perch's eye just before it is pecked out.

Melvill, cold in the tropical air, returns to the fire but finds it has grown weak in the meantime and there is no more driftwood for it to consume.

fourteen

~~~

Melvill awakes to Tinor's entreaties. The old woman keeps pointing at him and covering his nose. He remembers these gestures and strips off his clothes, removing his breeches while still under the sheet. She takes the pile, the fish smell clinging to them heavily. He awkwardly covers himself in the togalike sheet, leaving his left arm exposed and most of his right leg. His shoes are there by the mat but he chooses not to put them on. Melvill goes out of the hut into the bright day. It must be almost noon: he has slept all morning. The fishy taste of his breath assures him that his recollections of the night's proceedings are real.

The village is lazy and none of Marheyo's clan is in view. Melvill is acutely hungry. He recalls the bananas and other fruit in the hut but at the moment he has more pressing needs and walks toward the stream. There he is struck by how natural and comfortable the Typees' methods of toilet have become to him. He thinks of the privy in the afterhouse on the *Acushnet* and of carrying the sloshing stinking pot to the side of the ship as the whaler rolls and bucks on the ocean.

On his way back to Marheyo's hut to find something to eat Korykory intercepts him. He is with a group of his young friends—five dark men-boys lively and eager. Korykory insists that Melvill join them and they herd him along.

"I need to get something to eat—*kiki*—but I will join you later. Where will you be? At the Ti?"

They smile and chatter and continue to steer Melvill toward a jungle path. Two of the men-boys are carrying large earthen jugs; another has something wrapped in an old smudged sheet, about the size of a baby, which he holds pinned under one arm. Korykory is the tallest and strongest built of the young men— he is probably the eldest.

Melvill ceases his objections and goes with them. The path they begin is the one leading to the place of the cannibal ritual but soon they diverge onto a less traveled path, so narrow they form a singlefile line and still heavy waxy leaves continually thump against Melvill's exposed arm. They seem to be in a rush, which is not a normal pace for the Typees, unless going to war or to meet a trading ship. But they are not heading toward the mountains for an encounter with the Happars nor toward the sea.

They move through the jungle, Melvill in the middle of the line. The path is slightly uneven underfoot and Melvill wishes he had put on his shoes.

Suddenly there is an opening in the vegetation where several logs lie around a tree stump that is still rooted to the ground. The natives sit on the logs while the one with the shrouded object places it on the stump then removes the soiled cover with a jerk. It is a small statue, one of their myriad gods no doubt. This is a smiling beatific god. Its size and its grinning countenance make it a stark contrast to Boolaa, the god carved in the mountain, although the gray stone is the same.

This god is "Moa Artua," according to the young men, who keep repeating the name and patting the idol affectionately, like an old faithful dog. The flat nose and the square shoulders of the statue remind Melvill of the one guarding Marheyo's bamboo shrine, Marheyo's granite avatar. They were possibly rendered by the same artisan.

Melvill smiles and says the god's name to demonstrate his comprehension.

Korykory makes a few opening remarks; it seems almost

that he is introducing Melvill to the little god. Then the men-boys with the jugs drink from them and hand them off—one to Melvill. He immediately knows the scent of arva-wai, and it instantly twists his gut in recollection. Nevertheless he takes a bitter sip and passes the jug along.

The natives alternately tell stories or make claims, all sounding highly boastful. Often *Happar this* or *Happar that*. And the jugs are passed steadily. Melvill thinks about how much the Typees are defined by the Happars. Without their ancient enemies, the Typees would not be who they are. So if to have a life, one must have purpose—then the Happars are lifegiving to the Typees, and vice versa: ironic. Melvill thinks of the French encampment at Nukuheva Bay and their mounting encroachment. One day the Typees and Happars may have to join forces against a common enemy. Melvill takes another drink. That day—when that alliance is declared—both cultures will cease to exist. All the indigenous cultures of the island will cease in time. All the natives will be like Marnoo, an odd assortment of many tribes but not recognizably one tribe. Then inevitably the European blood will mix with the islanders'. No doubt it already has and the mixture courses through the veins of bastard children. Melvill takes another drink. And then what will there be here, in a generation? In two, three? Melvill sees an archipelago of European-island-not-European-not-island peoples. With no common culture to recall and to honor....

Melvill takes another drink. He aches for home.

He is suddenly sick of listening to the gibberish of Korykory and his friends. He stands off-balance and begins teetering down the path. Korykory calls to him—"Hermes! Hermes!"—but he does not respond and the islander does not try to stop him. The white sheet Melvill is wearing is in disarray and part of it drags on the ground. A shoot from some vegetation scratches his arm at the shoulder but Melvill barely notices, numb from the arva-wai.

Barefoot, he hurries along the path faster and faster, as if it is downhill and he is gaining momentum. His thoughts run to Fayaway. He sees her eating the fishes until he forces that image from his mind: instead the day she swam in the lake, her wet hair black and pressed closed to her head and neck and shoulders, her lovely face oval and radiant . . . then the watersnake coiled around her arm.

He shakes that picture out of his mind too.

Melvill emerges onto the more traveled path and immediately meets a pair of Typees, a couple, man and woman. They look at him strangely as he plunges past, still off balance on the level terrain. In New Bedford or New York City he could wander the crowded streets virtually unnoticed, all day all night, as if invisible. But here he is an oddity, a twoheaded toad, a flightless bird.

Melvill propels himself in the direction of Fayaway's hut, though he is disoriented and not at all certain of his course. He walks for what seems like a long while. At an intersection of paths he meets another Typee couple—this pair is young and Melvill imagines he knows their purpose in sneaking off to the jungle. He asks, "Fayaway? The home of Fayaway?"

They looked puzzled at first then the boy motions emphatically down the path that crosses to Melvill's right. The girl, pretty but not as pretty as Fayaway, agrees and motions emphatically too. It occurs to Melvill that they may be simply trying to rid themselves of him but he follows their direction nonetheless.

He strides along quickly, not quite so drunk now, his leg indicating no signs of distress. Melvill's sheet snags on something on the ground, and in freeing it with a hard jerk it rips. Now his toga is dirty, disheveled, torn. He continues on. At length the path ends at a settlement. Melvill stands in the clearing, unsure, then he determines that it is Fayaway's, but looking strange from this new perspective.

He gathers and straightens his tappa sheet as best he can and starts for Fayaway's hut. What time of day is it? he wonders.

The ubiquitous gang of children playing in the yard sees him coming and rushes to him, their brown feet kicking up brown dust. Before they even reach him they begin chattering in the negative: Fayaway is not in her hut?

"Where is she?" The children, a dozen or more, encircle him, some smiling and touching his ragged covering, worse than the mantle of a beggar. "Where is Fayaway?"

The children do not try to communicate a response even though they must know what he asks. In fact they are strangely silent. Melvill is befuddled, there at the center of these children, his head beginning to ache, his feet sore. He feels so exhausted that he is tempted to fall to the hard dusty ground and sleep there. Then there is a hand on his arm. A little girl is touching his shoulder where he has been cut. Blood is leaking from a superficial wound. The child looks into his eyes for a moment weighing something then she begins to lead him by the hand. A few of her playmates raise a protest but quickly stop; perhaps they are afraid of making too much noise.

The girl takes Melvill behind a row of huts and onto another jungle path which is narrow and rocky. Then Melvill realizes these are not rocks underfoot: the natives have placed seashells on the ground, broken apart and cracked from traffic. The sharp edges dig into his feet and Melvill misses the numbness of the arva-wai.

The way of shells only continues about twenty yards before becoming smooth again. The little girl stops and points ahead, unwilling to step beyond the broken shells. "Fayaway," she says as she rushes away, back across the seashells and out of sight.

Melvill is left alone there on the jungle path, his sheet dirty and torn, his arm, his feet, his head throbbing with pain—not even certain why he has been seeking Fayaway. But there is nothing left to do now except complete his quest. He continues on, holding his sheet around himself, like a city lady crossing a muddy, manured street, he thinks.

After a bend in the path Melvill finds a small bamboo hut

that has only three sides, not too dissimilar from the death shrines the Typees build their warriors. He thinks of Marheyo's recently completed shrine with its ugly little totem waiting patiently for the old man to perish. The floor of this three-sided hut is covered with strips of leaves, and there are gourds of food and water, folded tappa sheets too.

Fayaway is not there but in a moment Melvill hears a rustling in the jungle and he realizes there is an ill-defined path there. Not paying attention, Fayaway is fully in the small clearing before she realizes Melvill is there. She is speechless but only for a moment—soon she is ranting at him, angry and afraid, her voice strange with tears. Melvill does not know what to say or do, so he stands there absorbing her hurt and hostility. She steps toward him as she continues to rail. When she is close he instinctively reaches out to her; doing so, his tattered sheet falls to the ground. He holds her close and she continues to scold him, not as vehemently now and seemingly without purpose. Her breath is hot on his shoulder. Fayaway stops when he kisses her forehead. Through the strands of her long dark hair he can feel the bones of her back. It is like holding a cat, he realizes, very much all skin and angular bones. Against his stomach he can sense the soft rises of her breasts. She reaches around and hugs him.

Though she says nothing her breath is still hot and sticky on his shoulder. They stand there for a long while. Melvill hears the caw of exotic birds, some distant, others close by. He cannot help but think of Genesis, of Adam and Eve: *The man and his wife were both naked, yet they felt no shame.* He listens for the slither of the Serpent.

He notices a scent, strange but not wholly unfamiliar. Similar to the bedding of Madeline, the New Bedford prostitute, and to the smell of the privy at home sometimes after his mother or sisters had finished.

He wishes he had a father. An older brother is not the same. But the thought is fleeting as Melvill feels his arousal prod up against Fayaway—suddenly a third party with them in the jungle, singleminded, intense. She feels it too and her body tenses. They continue to hold each other, Melvill bobbing against Fayaway's coarseness.

Fayaway then looks up and kisses Melvill on the lips, and drops to her knees. She stares at Melvill as if it is a strange creature just arrived in the clearing, the Serpent come after all. Melvill's heart is pounding so that he is short of wind. She quickly kisses it—

Melvill lifts her to her feet: "Not this way, my sweet girl." He picks her up, she weighs nothing, and carries her to the leafy floor of the hut.

She is happy there. They are happy there.

When they are finished Melvill rolls onto his back keeping his fingers lightly on Fayaway's face. He cannot grasp her feelings. She looks older, her hair matted, her cheeks and upper lip, tattooed with the two dots, damp with perspiration. It is not until he hears the hum of tiny flying insects that Melvill realizes he has dark sticky blood from his knees to his stomach.

Fayaway looks away, ashamed.

"It's all right," he says but the smell is beginning to nauseate him. He retrieves the dirty tappa sheet and attempts to clean himself; it does little good however.

Fayaway, still avoiding his eyes, offers him a gourd of water. He manages only to smear the gore in wider circles on his skin. He thinks of Karky and what the tattoo artisan might say about such a horrific design. Melvill's penis looks as if it has been attacked and injured. The winged insects swarm around it.

He realizes Fayaway is crying silent tears. Blood is on her thighs and her flat dimpled stomach. "It's all right," he repeats and kisses her salty cheek. "I'll be back. I promise."

He knows that she does not understand. He arranges his torn, dirty, bloodstained toga and begins down the path. He recalls his headache, and his scratched arm. He looks at the wound hopefully: Is it believable that so much blood came from the scratch? Of course not.

The path's broken shells prick painfully at his feet. He steps lightly. When Melvill emerges into the area of huts the children are still playing but they disregard him. Even the little girl who led him to Fayaway. Melvill wants to reach Marheyo's hut and the bathing stream by some obscure little-traveled path but he only knows the one way, back through the Ti grove, which will no doubt be busy this time of day. The sun is high.

He asks for a sudden torrential rain, a regular happening on the island. No god is responding—neither his nor any of the myriad carved idols all around. The sky remains its unyielding tropical blue.

Melvill makes it beyond the cluster of huts and onto the next path. He thinks of poor Fayaway in the jungle—bloodied, ashamed, and no doubt feeling totally alone. He vows to return to her as quickly as possible. Might she become pregnant? He envisions a little boy or girl half his and half island beauty. He thinks of the half French bastards at Nukuheva Bay and he feels guilt. He assures himself that Fayaway cannot become pregnant now. Again he wishes for a father.

He continues along the path. He imagines that he must look like some ancient Greek beggar, or a traveler who has been robbed and left for dead on the road, or perhaps a survivor of the Trojan War, a poet caught unaware on the battlefield. The smell that emanates from him however is not man sweat and horse sweat and warrior blood nobly spilled, though there is something of each of those in the pungent scent.

Melvill longs for the cooling waters of the stream and for his comfortable mat in Marheyo's home. His thoughts are interrupted by voices calling from somewhere ahead on the path: "Hermes! Hermes!"

Impulsively Melvill crashes through the thick jungle vegetation and crouches still on the ground, hiding.

Breathing as silently as possible, he estimates that two or three minutes elapse before the two young warriors pass him.

He can barely see them through the leaves and vines but they might be from the cadre that guarded Toby when they first arrived in the valley. How long now? Can it only have been a few weeks? Damn you, Toby. The warriors call his name again. Korykory must assume he is lost and has his people out searching. Or Fayaway's violation has been discovered and there is an angry mob out looking for him. No—word cannot travel so fast in the valley, he feels certain.

Melvill waits another few minutes before leaving his hiding place and continuing on. He chides himself for acting like a criminal and avoiding the searchers. It's best not to try to explain anything. Let them concoct their own theories regarding his whereabouts. He knows that round the turn there is a crossing of paths, thus multiplying his chances of encountering more searchers. He is surprised by how familiar he has become with the maze of paths, to know what lies ahead.

By the time he hears them it is too late. . . .

Mowmow, the one-eyed captain, and two warriors are standing face to face with Melvill—all four equally surprised. Melvill feels Mowmow's solitary eye probing him, the Typee explaining Melvill's appearance to his own satisfaction.

Melvill is afraid.

The warrior captain, who is wearing a colorful cape of feathers, speaks calmly to his men and they instantly seize Melvill. He is too surprised to shout in protest. They take him along one of the cross paths. "Let me go. What are you doing?" Mowmow does not respond but the half smile on his lips, strangely contorting his face and emphasizing his bull's-eye, heightens Melvill's anxiety. He has seen that expression: Taggart, aboard the *Acushnet* right before he had young Jones flogged, navystyle, for "thiefing" he said, and "b'havior ins'bord'nate." It was only a few days later that Jones was lost, fallen overboard during a perfectly peaceful watch. Melvill recalls the search boats circling aft, their lanterns like luminous eyes of seamonsters in the dark.

When they are far from the main path Mowmow commands his warriors to stop. They continue to firmly hold Melvill by the arms. He tries to keep himself from trembling. Mowmow continues to look him over with his eye, the singularity of which makes it all the more terrifying, then begins sniffing Melvill, Mowmow's broad nose actually twitching like a huntingdog's. His flaring nostrils move along Melvill's chest and stomach. All at once Mowmow snatches the sheet away.

Melvill is standing there naked and shrunken, the blood dried rustbrown. He thinks of the color of the ocean when a whale has been mortally harpooned and its salty blood flows out into the salty ocean, ashes to ashes.

"It isn't what you think," Melvill says quietly and stupidly. He tries halfheartedly to break free from the warriors' grip.

Mowmow, who looks ridiculously ceremonial in the cape of feathers, begins speaking in scratchy ominous tones then reaches behind his back, under the feather cape, and brings forth a longbladed knife.

In Melvill's mind flash stories of natives' circumcision rituals. He wills himself not to lose control of his bowel. "I intended no harm . . . she is not harmed in fact . . . Fayaway is just fine . . . Talk to Fayaway—"

Her name elicits a reaction from Mowmow. He looks into Melvill's eyes, the Typee's eye darting from side to side; then he stares at Melvill's bloodied organ. Fayaway's name seems to have fractured his resolve. Before Mowmow can recover his will the name "Hermes!" is called from somewhere along the path, ahead or behind.

When the name is called again, Melvill responds, "Yes—yes, I'm here!" He feels the warriors' grip loosen. Melvill breaks free and runs down the path, not sure where he is going other than away from Mowmow and his long knife. He hears the captain give orders to his young warriors and Melvill senses they are pursuing him. He has perhaps a fifty-yard lead and feels strong, the blood pumping hard through his body. He can

run all day if necessary.

He hears "Hermes!" a third time, closer now. It might be Korykory or it might be some other group of islanders out to retaliate Fayaway's violation. Or perhaps it is Korykory out to revenge her violation.

Melvill's wind is coming easily to him. His legs are working in a furious but smooth rhythm. His bare feet, their tenderness vanished, touch lightly on the jungle path. His bloodstained part thumps up and down, its furious rhythm equal to his legs.

At the crossing of paths Melvill notices a group of three Typees to his left—maybe they were calling to him. They do shout as he flies past . . . no, the sound is not right . . . some other group is shouting . . . behind? . . . to the right? Is the whole damned cannibal nation hunting for him? Running, running, Melvill risks a glance backward. Mowmow's warriors have stopped to consult the other group. Melvill runs harder still to exploit their halting. He sees a path, narrower and lesser used, that splits from the main thoroughfare. On impulse he takes the new path, hoping it will confuse whatever pursuit remains. Immediately he senses that this way slopes downhill.

When he feels he is out of view he stops. Listens. Tries to master his breathing. Looks behind along the narrow path. Through the vegetation he can barely see the summit of a mountain the islanders call "Kweekway," which gives him some general idea of his location. If he is correct he has taken a series of paths that have led more or less toward the coast. But he is far from Marheyo's hut and farther still from Fayaway, in her temporary feminine exile.

Melvill recalls the shack of firearms near the ocean. It is the only logical place to go. If the old old man is still its only sentinel, Melvill should at least be able to arm himself. He thinks especially of the Wheeler revolving flintlock.

Against the entire cannibal nation? He pushes the question from his mind, there is no use for it.

He moves on, hoping he is correct about his general

direction, hoping he will soon feel the fresh salt air on his skin. He loves the ocean, even when it is the color of death. It is a shame that one must sign on with a den of thieves in order to sail. That one must risk more than one's safety. He sees Taggart's rat face; he hears the sounds in the dark storeroom, young Jones no doubt terrified and burning with humiliation— his sullenness afterward, a soul rented like cracked earth, then his *unaccountable* death: fallen overboard during his watch, on a calm night, the southern hemisphere stars glittering like distant torches, the moon a waning crescent in the boundless sky.

The path descends steeply and feeds into a wider one. Melvill hesitates. He listens for any human noises. There is only wind in his ears . . . and the cry of a gull. Then he is close. The ocean must lie to his right. Melvill steps into the open. The terrain is similar to the sea path he has taken before but it is not that path, he feels certain. He commits to finishing his journey to the ocean. Perhaps it shall end there.

Melvill stands at the edge of the rugged terrain before the path slopes down finally to the beach. The quickest route to the guns would be to descend to the beach and walk the quarter mile (half mile?) to the main sea path then proceed up to the shack. However that would leave a great distance to travel in plain view. Suspecting his destination, Typees may already be on the beach. Would they not also suspect the gun shack? Melvill will not allow himself to ponder the question.

The only route then is between the hillocks to his left, which are like a pod of whales surfacing on the plain. His hope is that he will find himself very near the shack when he reaches the end of the hillocks.

The sun is hot on his shoulders as he begins the serpentine path through the green hillocks, each rising so gently and sloping so perfectly, as if a manmade mount, and each high enough to obstruct his view of the ocean. Melvill can hear the surf though and the scores of seabirds calling forlornly to sea.

He thinks of Coleridge's albatross, and that he is so exhausted it feels like a heavy weight is strung about his neck. His mind wanders and he imagines himself in a boat among this pod of whales. The ground seems to pitch beneath his feet. He envisions harpoons protruding from the humpbacks. And the blood pouring out and pouring out, an endless quantity spilled into the bottomless ocean. The blood rolls down the hillocks forming a crimson stream where Melvill walks; the ground is almost slippery with whale gore. . . .

The series of hillocks is longer than Melvill anticipated but they finally end and the open plain is before him. He can see the weathered gray shack, perhaps two hundred yards distant. Melvill crouches in the wiry grass—no one appears to be here. Better to sneak his way to the shack, or to run across the open field? There is no way to sneak per se, other than to crawl the two hundred yards on his belly, his bare sunburned bloodstained belly.

Run it is.

As soon as he is in the open the ocean breeze hits him in full, the salt smell in the fresh cool air. And another scent, familiar, but his brain will not place it. Melvill reaches the shack and stops himself against the grayplanked wall. He breathes hard pressing himself flat against the shack—a splinter pricks his backside. He moves cautiously to the corner of the shack and peers up the path. No one is there. Perhaps the natives have not inferred his whereabouts after all. He hurries into the shack hoping the ancient Typee guardian is not there; but he is. Sitting as placidly and as obliviously as ever. Melvill stands there looking at him for a moment before going to the guns. He looks for the best piece, the Wheeler revolving flintlock. For a few seconds he cannot find it, then it is there propped in a corner.

"You are lucky, old fellow," Melvill says to the aged warrior as he inspects the bulky firearm. "Your world is no doubt the one you recall from your youth. You sit there all day running through grassy fields and being with your first maiden." The barrel and the stock are fine. He looks for .52-caliber ammunition. "So what if you soil yourself here in this place. Your other place, inside your mind, is what matters." He finds the ammunition and begins loading the cylinder which allows seven shots before reloading, a mechanical marvel. It sticks a little at first then works freely. "The fruit is always sweet, the opponents always easy, the maidens always accommodating— and you must always have your family about you, parents, grandparents, children, children's children—a family picnic every day." Melvill is surprised when he feels a tear trickle down his cheek. There are serviceable pistols but he has no way of carrying one, nor extra ammunition for that matter.

Now what? He has achieved his goal of arming himself. Now what?

If he can reach Marheyo's hut surely the old man and Korykory will provide him asylum—unless they know about Fayaway and are angry too. He thinks of her there alone in the jungle. He can only see the dark, almost black, gore on her thighs. And smell its smell. Clearly Korykory is attracted to Fayaway, perhaps thinking of marrying her. Now. . . . Melvill must not contemplate it. Returning to Marheyo's family seems to be his only option.

Melvill stands in the doorway of the shack for a moment and looks back at the old warrior. "Enjoy the remainder of your reverie, my friend. It will end soon enough."

Melvill steps out into the world holding the loaded flintlock. Gulls cry overhead. The wind blows his hair and beard. Again that scent on the breeze, a scent from an unsettling dream. He is only a few yards from the shack when he sees the first natives on the hill. Melvill stands frozen, his mind thinking of everything and nothing at once, thoughts fly past but none catch in the webwork.

He finally decides to run back into the shack but it is too late: they have seen him and the shack is no fortification.

Desperately he tries to identify the Typees, who are now hurrying toward him, less than a quarter mile. There are a dozen or more. And another group coming over the rise. The first group is close enough that he recognizes Mowmow, his feathered cape flapping in the wind.

Melvill readies his weapon. "Stop! Stop now!" He levels the Wheeler at the advancing group. But they continue. "Stop. Now!" Without intending to, his tense finger squeezes the trigger and the explosive shot rings out. The gun bucks against his shoulder, and the cloud of smoke disappears on the wind.

None of the Typees fall as if hit but they all crouch low to the ground, all except Mowmow who continues his pace unimpressed by Melvill's flintlock. Melvill manually advances the cylinder and fires again, again not taking specific aim. Mowmow has his knife in hand, his stride is murderously purposeful. His bull's-eye seems luminous among his dark features.

Melvill is trembling as the next shot is fired. It is on target enough to remove two feathers from Mowmow's cape—green and white they flutter in the air.

Now Mowmow is close enough that Melvill cannot miss— and the captain's mortality seems finally to cross his mind. He stops, holding but not raising the knife.

Melvill is breathing hard but cannot catch his breath. The flintlock barrel bobs up and down slightly. He stares down the site with one eye, in line with Mowmow's tattooed target. His finger feels the trigger, knows how little pressure is needed to end Mowmow's life, toys with the pressure. He wonders if Mowmow's shrine is built, or if it might become the work of his relatives.

He feels the trigger. . . .

"Melvill?" a voice calls. "Herman Melvill?" The wind has twisted the words. Their origin is uncertain, perhaps his own overtaxed imagination. "Herman Melvill!" Up the hill standing erect among the crouched figures, three men—and one is dressed as a white man dresses, as a sailor dresses. "Don't kill the bastard, my boy!" The sailor has an accent, British maybe or Australian. The three men continue the descent. Meanwhile Melvill continues to watch Mowmow, who has not turned to see the new arrivals. Perhaps he knows of them already, or perhaps he is too intent on spilling Melvill's blood.

As the three men come down the hill—Korykory and the native ambassador Marnoo are with the sailor—the Typees begin to stand and relax, no longer afraid of Melvill's shooting them. The sailor is an older man with white in his hair and beard, a striped shirt and blue trousers.

That smell—Melvill knows it now. He turns toward the sea and there it sits at anchor in the bay, a squarerigged whaleship, slightly smaller than the *Acushnet*. The smell which had sickened him for so many months now is the sweet scent of survival, of liberation. *Deus ex machina*, he thinks incredulously.

Too late he hears "Watch yer back, boy!" Mowmow has knocked him to the ground. The Wheeler has discharged pointlessly as it flies from his hands. Melvill is only able to roll onto his back before Mowmow has him pinned and his knife at his throat. His eye bores into Melvill's skull like a shipwright's drill. The tip of Mowmow's knife pierces his skin. Melvill feels the blood trickle down the side of his neck. For the moment Mowmow does not puncture more deeply.

The sailor is close now. Korykory and Marnoo are speaking to Mowmow, Korykory excitedly, Marnoo calmly slowly.

The Typee captain holds the knife point in Melvill's skin. Melvill says nothing as he waits for death or life. He thinks of nothing, not of his past or his future. His mind is a mirror reflecting only what he sees: Mowmow's disfigured face framed by the bluest sky . . . a sailor's dream of a sky—

Melvill thinks of his prey for so many months, of the magnificent whales, rising from the depths for life's breath and being greeted with a harpoon in the back, then a second and a third, their red blood pouring forth as they struggle against the unprovoked attack, tugging the whale boats through the waves, the men laughing like children on a toboggan in the snow, until finally no energy is left, a lung pierced, the liver, maybe the brain itself, and the giant corpse can be dragged to the ship to be dissected and processed, another life ended at sea. . . .

—Mowmow withdraws the knifeblade, gets up from Melvill and slowly walks away.

The sailor helps Melvill stand. "I'm secondmate on the *Lucy Ann* there." He leads Melvill toward a dinghy on the beach; already the tide is going out. "We've had a rough time of it— sickness and a freak storm drowned twelve good men—we're desperate for harpooners specially. We happened to cross the *London Packet* and a Tobias Greene told us his tale, said you was in need of rescuing as much as we need of men with whaling knowhow." They are at the dinghy and the Australian is pushing it into the waves. "Get in, mate. Best be takin no more time."

Melvill steps into the boat mechanically. The Aussie gets the dinghy on the water and hops in. "Grab an oar and we'll be aboard in no time."

Melvill does as he is told and puts his back into the stroke.

"My lord, mate, you're a sight. That lad who speaks some English and me been scourin the whole devil valley lookin for you. Half the Typee out to look too."

Korykory has come down to the water's edge. He raises a hand but Melvill keeps moving the oars. Beyond Korykory is the hill with its worn path leading out of sight. Beyond the hill not even the mountains are in view. Somewhere in that verdant nothingness is Fayaway. He tries to recall her face but her features will not come to him. He can only recall the heat of her bloody sex, the taste of her sweaty skin. Korykory is still standing watching, just a manshape on the beach now, not even waving, motionless as driftwood.

"There be a slicker under the seat, mate—best be putting it on."

Melvill finds the long coat in a wad. It is foul with sweat and sea salt, whale gore and lord knows what else. He slips it on and buckles it tight; it's a fair fit.

When they reach the starboard side of the *Lucy Ann* Melvill glances back one final time and the manshape is retreating. In a moment it will be gone for good. Melvill takes the ropeladder in his hands and looks heavenward. The sailors peering back are black against the blinding tropical sky, mere featureless shadows staring over the gunwale.

Melvill begins to climb, as the small boat bucks beneath him on the eternally restless waves.

a conversation
with the author

by Beth Gilstrap

On a gray March evening (in 2011), I spoke with Ted Morrissey, author of the novel *Men of Winter* (originally published in 2010) and the forthcoming novella and story collection *Weeping with an Ancient God*. We talked about the publishing industry—and the joys and terrors of writing. (Note that *Weeping* was supposed to come out in the summer of 2012, as part of a collection of stories, but its publisher went out of business on the verge of its release.)

What was your impression on the response you received to Men of Winter? *How do you feel about being compared to Tolstoy and Homer?*

Being published by a new, small press, Punkin House, there have been no formal reviews of *Men of Winter* yet, so the reactions have come from actual readers—who seem to like it very much. Among my various jobs, I work part-time at my small-town library, so it's interesting to see the novel's coming and going (so far its going has been pretty regular), and people who realize I'm the author will remark that they liked it. Of course, if they didn't, they probably wouldn't say anything period. A local book club is planning on its being one of their summer readings and on having me come in to read and chat with the members—which should be fun.

The comparisons to Tolstoy and Homer are very flattering of course, but I know they're based more on setting and plot, and not on storytelling ability per se. Ironically, I hadn't read much Tolstoy, much at all, when I wrote the novel, but for the past year I've been reading the Russians a lot, including Tolstoy. Somehow I missed much of Russian literature in my formal education, so I'm trying to catch up. In the summer and fall I read shorter works by Dostoevsky, Turgenev, and Gogol; then this winter I read *Anna Karenina* and have just recently begun *War and Peace*, which is going to take me a very long time.

Homer I know well, especially the *Odyssey* as I've been teaching it every fall for fifteen years now, and I've used several translations, including Robert Fitzgerald's, which is where I took the title from, his translation of Book 11, Odysseus' journey to the underworld.

What inspired you to write Men of Winter?

I actually began writing what would become the novel about thirteen years ago; I finished the book in three years; then it took me ten years (and two literary agents, both of whom gave up in despair about the industry) to find a publisher—my point is I'm not sure I can recall specific inspiration. I'd written a short story as a sequel to Mary Shelley's *Frankenstein* ("A Wintering Place," which eventually found a home at *Eleven Eleven*), and I liked that story a lot. So I decided to write another short piece based on another book I loved, and for whatever reason I started thinking about the *Odyssey*. I've always found Calypso the most sympathetic character in the poem, as her love for Odysseus is totally disregarded by the council of gods and goddesses who decide that the hero should be allowed to go home. I guess it was my thinking about brokenhearted Calypso that started me moving in the direction that wound up with my writing the novel.

In Men of Winter, *you have a journalist/poet narrator; why would you say writers make interesting subjects?*

I like writing in first-person—though I know that mode has been taking a lot of criticism for some time now—and to me it doesn't make sense that someone who isn't a writer of some sort would be able to write well enough to tell a whole novel-length story (I know that's condescending and there are people who write well who aren't writers per se—and I've written first-person stories with non-writers as their narrators). Also, I grew up around the newspaper business and worked as a sports reporter for seven years, so I feel like I have an affinity for newspapering and newspapermen. His being a poet, I suppose, is a nod to Homer.

I tend to like novels and stories whose main characters are writers, but that's because I can relate to them. I'm not sure journalists/writers as main characters are inherently interesting. No matter who or what your main character is, hopefully you can find a way to make his or her situation of interest to the reader.

What were some of the high points and low points of writing either Men of Winter *or* Weeping with an Ancient God?

I actually wrote *Weeping with an Ancient God* before *Men of Winter*, and my understanding, from researching the market, was that I'd have trouble finding a publisher for the novella-length manuscript. My contacts with publishers and agents bore that out: no one had any interest in publishing something shorter than a novel from a no-name author. So I squirreled the manuscript away and set about trying to write something longer, which ended up being *Men of Winter*, even though my original notion was that it'd be another short story.

The high points, besides the process of writing them—which I genuinely do enjoy (even though it's hard work at times)—have of course been finding people who like them and who want to publish them. During those ten to fifteen years that I was having trouble finding a publisher for my books, the industry changed because publishing technology changed. On the one hand, it's harder than ever to publish with a name house (unless they're going to make a million dollars off your book, they don't have the time of day for you), but on-demand technology has made it feasible to publish authors in small enough press runs to make it profitable, thus giving rise to many, many small presses.

My lowest points were of course the innumerable rejections I received from publishers, often via an agent. The biggest disappointment came when I'd been contacted by a literary agent because she'd read one of my stories in *Glimmer Train Stories*, and she wanted to know if I had a book-length manuscript. I said yes, I had the novella manuscript (*Weeping*), and she didn't even want to see it; but I'd also just started working on what would become *Men of Winter*, so she said to send it to her when I was finished with it. It took me three years to complete it, and the whole time I had in mind that an agent was waiting to read it. When I finished, I tracked her down (she'd moved to a different agency), and she wanted to read it—but then she declined to represent it. That was very disappointing.

In anticipation of *Weeping with an Ancient God* being published by Punkin House [which was set to happen in the summer of 2012, but the press went out of business before bringing it out], I sent the first chapter out as a stand-alone piece titled "Melvill in the Marquesas," and it was picked up very quickly by *The Final Draft*—and to my surprise I received four other offers of publication (even though I'd withdrawn the manuscript elsewhere immediately), and two rejections that were very complimentary. To be honest, I thought the excerpt in particular was so quirky it might take me quite a while to find a journal to take it. But editors have responded very enthusiastically to it, which has been, frankly, both surprising and vindicating.

What inspired you to write about Herman Melville's encounter with cannibals in the Marquesas Islands?

I'd been a Melville fan for quite a while, even though I hadn't read, at the time, a lot of his work. I always admired that he abandoned the style of writing that would have made him a wealthy man (the sort of writing he did in *Typee* and *Omoo*) and experimented with other forms (especially *Moby-Dick*) that led to the reading public's abandoning him. His last several works were self-published in fact. In particular, though, A&E had a *Great Books Festival* and featured some of the world's greatest works of literature and their authors; it was narrated by Donald Sutherland.

One of the episodes was about Melville and his writing of *Moby-Dick*, and it painted him as a tragic figure, consumed by financial troubles and self-doubt and all kinds of personal and family problems. Yet he didn't do the "easy" thing and write popular stories that would have solved many of his problems, especially his financial ones. From the A&E program, I also learned that it was when he was a young sailor that he first heard the whaling legend that eventually inspired him to write *Moby-Dick*. I started researching Melville's biography, and I read *Typee*, his own fictionalized account of his cannibal adventure —and I soon realized it could make a great story in itself.

But I didn't want it to be a biography of Melville per se; I wanted it to be a genuine work of fiction (dare I say, a genuine work of art). So I did a few things to distance my story from its being a biography, in my way of thinking anyway: I'd discovered that his family name was originally spelled "Melvill" without the "e," so I thought it'd be an interesting twist to use his original name that was not as well known, in fact barely known at all. Also, I was going through something of a Hemingway phase at the time, so I decided to write about Melville in a very spare and modern style, in contrast to his own richly florid and poetic prose, thus firmly transplanting his nineteenth-century story into the twentieth century (now, twenty-first century).

How did you get interested in "revisionist fiction"? What are the beauties and complications of working in this genre?

I'm not sure how I became interested in revisionist fiction exactly, other than I read several examples of it that I really, really enjoyed and admired (coming to mind are J. M. Coetzee's *Foe*, Jean Rhys's *Wide Sargasso Sea*, Valerie Martin's *Mary Reilly*, John Updike's *Gertrude and Claudius*). Having been a life-long bibliophile (bibliomaniac more accurately), the idea of taking characters and settings that I loved and working within their frames and conventions myself was just very appealing, like getting to spend terrific quality time with beloved friends and family.

One of the beauties of doing revisionist fiction, then, is just getting to spend all that intellectual time with an author and his/her characters, etc. I'm not a musician, but I suppose it's a bit like doing a cover of a song that you love—changing it up and making it yours, but because you love and respect the original so much, not because you think the original failed in some way and you want to do a better version. I enjoy playing with the nuances of the original, isolating certain aspects of the tone or imagery, for example, and amplifying it or recoloring it or recasting it somehow; or emphasizing an aspect of characterization that is only hinted at in the original . . . the possibilities are truly endless.

I like to write in a way that makes it unnecessary for my reader to have read the original to make sense of the story—I'm sure, for instance, that there are people who have read *Men of Winter* who've never read the *Iliad* or the *Odyssey* so they don't get any of the allusions, but yet (hopefully) they understand and enjoy it on its own terms. On the other hand, if my reader does have some level of familiarity with the original text, it should enrich their reading experience, and maybe even get them to think about the original work in a way they hadn't before.

What type of research did you do in preparation for this type of writing?

For *Weeping with an Ancient God*, I read a lot of Melville and about Melville. I read with special care his novel *Typee*, which was his own thinly veiled fictional account of his time in the Marquesas Islands. It's important to say, though, that while I used his biography and *Typee* for inspiration, and for period details, I wasn't interested in being faithful to what really happened. There are some episodes that appear in his novel as well, and some things that his biographers discuss, but I felt at liberty to change those episodes and to add wholly original material as my own story needed them. I also did some research on the whaling industry, like the actual process of hunting whales, and on whaling towns like Nantucket and New Bedford—again for inspiration and period details, not in an effort to teach my readers about whaling, and so forth.

Men of Winter was a bit different, in terms of research. Even though it's strongly implied to be set in early-twentieth-century Russia, Siberia in fact, I deliberately avoided pinning it down to a specific time and place. I wanted the narrative to have one foot in the "real" world, and one foot in some other sort of world. I've also tried to accomplish that feel via some other narrative techniques that so far no one has seemed to notice—which either means I did them so well that they're invisible, or that I did them so poorly that they in fact accomplished nothing. I already knew the *Iliad* pretty well and *Odyssey* very well, like the back of my hand, to employ a cliché, so I didn't have to read them especially for this project—they're a part of me like my own family history—but I did research what life in Siberia was like, and I researched European history in the first decades of the twentieth century, especially World War I warfare, and other mechanical technologies.

But I also made a lot of stuff up. I've had a few readers compliment me on my thorough research, which implies to me that they think all of the geographical and period details are genuine, when in fact there are very few details that I included straight from my research. So I do take such comments as a compliment, but not to my thorough research so much as to my ability to write made-up stuff that sounds real. In essence, they're complimenting me at being an accomplished liar. To which I nod demurely and say "Thank you."

~~~~~

Beth Gilstrap has been awarded residencies at the Vermont Studio Center and the Cabin at Shotpouch Creek through Oregon State University's Spring Creek Project for ideas, nature and the written word. Her work has appeared in *Quiddity, Ambit, Minnesota Review, Superstition Review,* and *Twisted South,* among others. She lives in Charlotte, North Carolina, with her husband and their many rescue pets. Visit at bethgilstrap.com.

about the illustrator

Adam Perschbacher is a member of the Central Illinois arts community, and among the founding members of The Pharmacy co-op and gallery. Though predominantly a painter and builder of large geometric abstractions (which he deems "Objects"), Perschbacher maintains an equal and often more recognizable penchant for illustration and graphic design. He has a bachelors in Visual Art from the University of Illinois Springfield and works as a designer for Hanson Professional Services, Inc. He has hosted five solo exhibitions featuring his geometric Objects as well as co-hosted numerous group exhibitions across Springfield. Visit agpgallery. com for more information.

about the author

Ted Morrissey is the author of the novels *Men of Winter* and *An Untimely Frost*, the novelette *Figures in Blue,* and stories and essays in more than thirty journals, including *Glimmer Train, PANK, Writers Ask* and the *North American Review*. A Ph.D. in English studies, he has also published *The* Beowulf *Poet and His Real Monsters*, winner of the D. Simon Evans Prize for distinguished scholarship. He is an adjunct lecturer in English at the University of Illinois Springfield, and he is on the masthead of *Quiddity* literary journal as a fiction reader. He and his wife Melissa, also an educator, live near Springfield, Illinois. Together they have five adult children and a rescued silky terrier named Einstein. Visit at tedmorrissey.com, and follow @t_morrissey.

Photo by Melissa Morrissey

a note on the type

The book is set in Adobe Minion Pro. Minion is a digital type-face designed by Robert Slimbach for Adobe Systems in 1990, and Minion Pro was added to the family of typefaces in 2000. Minion was inspired by Renaissance-era type. The titles of the book are set in Poor Richard, which was designed by Paul Hickson, based on a Keystone Type Foundry design of about 1919.

www.ingramcontent.com/pod-product-compliance
Lightning Source LLC
Chambersburg PA
CBHW030229180626
46810CB00008B/3047